The author, Renee Week

an old murder mystery movie or reading a book on an intriguing whodunit, and that book will more likely than not include a touch of romance. Writing a novel was always on her bucket list and eventually, it became a reality. When not absorbed in the latest gripping murder plot, Renee is an associate editor/writer for a business publication and a professor who teaches graduate and undergraduate business courses, loves cooking, working out, and otherwise spends far too much time at the computer. She lives in rural Minnesota with her husband, Australian Shepherd, and an assortment of cats.

To Tim – my husband, my inspiration, my champion.

Renee Weeks

FALL FROM GRACE: FOR WHOM THE BELL TOLLS

AUSTIN MACAULEY PUBLISHERS™

LONDON • CAMBRIDGE • NEW YORK • SHARJAH

Copyright © Renee Weeks (2021)

Ordering Information
Quantity sales: Special discounts are available on quantity purchases by corporations, associations, and others. For details, contact the publisher at the address below.

Publisher's Cataloging-in-Publication data
Weeks, Renee
Fall from Grace: For Whom the Bell Tolls

ISBN 9781647501624 (Paperback)
ISBN 9781647501617 (Hardback)
ISBN 9781647501631 (ePub e-book)

Library of Congress Control Number: 2020916533

www.austinmacauley.com/us

First Published (2021)
Austin Macauley Publishers LLC
40 Wall Street, 33rd Floor, Suite 3302
New York, NY 10005
USA

mail-usa@austinmacauley.com
+1 (646) 5125767

I have to start by thanking my husband, Tim. From reading early drafts to giving me his opinions on the final version, he was as important to this book getting done as I was. Thank you so much, my dear. I am eternally grateful to my daughter, Desiree, for her encouragement, honest critiques, and support during this entire writing journey.

Chapter 1

George Martin never meant to cause problems for anyone— really. He had only wanted a couple of drinks after work before going home. He knew that if he had more than that, his wife would kill him—probably, literally. But one thing leads to another and, of course, you know what happened; he had more than two. It was quite understandable, therefore, that when he staggered out of the bar in downtown Glendale, that he should not have been driving a car.

George managed to unlock the car door and fell into the driver's seat. After some fumbling, he finally got the key into the ignition and took off. He always took the same route home—he knew no cops would be patrolling the street that went by the Catholic Church. He had never had an accident nor been caught for drunk driving and he was sure before long, he would be safely poured into bed by his wife.

As he swerved down the avenue that connected to Abbey Street, he was thinking about his wife. Elaine was such a peach, always there for him, always so patient even though he sometimes came home just a bit tipsy. Lately, though, she had been less than patient. She had threatened to leave him if he didn't stop his drinking. He was just wondering if maybe she was right, and he should cut down and spend more time with her when his thoughts were suddenly interrupted by the unusual direction his drive home had taken. He found his car somehow traveling at high speed across the immaculate lawn of the Our Lady of the Lake Catholic Church.

George tried to stop the damn thing. But although he tried and tried, he couldn't—it had a mind of its own! When it came to rest, it had managed to thoroughly destroy three flower beds, two rose bushes, and had remodeled a major chunk out of the bell tower. George no longer had a problem with alcohol; in fact, George no longer had problems of any kind. For you see, the bell tolled for George—George was dead.

***

Police Chief Carter McGraw sat at his cluttered desk sipping his coffee. He grimaced and thought, *Who made this stuff?* It tasted like tar heated up. He dumped the cup into the wastebasket and coffee splashed onto the floor and onto his pant leg. *Damn!* He just wanted to get through another day, which meant another day closer to retirement for him. Chief McGraw had been with the Glendale Police Department for nearly 30 years and he was getting tired. His hair was now gray—what there was of it—and his stomach was getting bigger every year. He had turned into a soft, wrinkled old man. All he wanted was to retire, go fishing, and try to avoid the chores his wife always had for him. He was just wondering how he would be able to accomplish that feat when his sergeant walked in.

Sergeant Walker tossed a report onto his desk and fell into the chair across and said, "Another drunk driver got it last night, Chief. Wouldn't you think they would learn by now?"

Chief McGraw shrugged his shoulders and reached for the report and replied, "Some things never change." He read, "The driver of the vehicle was a George Martin, age 47, address 302 Maplewood, DOA."

Sergeant Walker explained with a grin, "This one's a bit different, Chief; the guy wound up crashing into the bell tower of the Catholic Church."

***

The bulldozer hummed steadily as it slowly knocked down the leftovers from George Martin's late-night drive. Each trip back and forth to the waiting dump truck took a bite out of the remains of what had been a landmark at Our Lady's for nearly a quarter of a century. People gathered and found themselves fascinated by the process. Finally, all that remained was the last chunk of the tower base. Everyone started to scatter; there was nothing more to see.

Suddenly, the bulldozer stopped, and the driver jumped off and then ran down into the hole. He started yelling excitedly, "Call the police, someone—I think I just found myself a body!"

***

As Chief McGraw drove to the Catholic Church, his mind turned back in time to 25 years ago. That is just about how long the church has been in existence. What was going on at that time? Who could have been buried beneath the bell tower? *Damn, this would happen just as I was about to retire. Why can't people just behave?* He arrived at the scene just in time to see the forensic guys doing their stuff. A couple of guys were measuring while others were labeling and taking photos. The medical examiner, Dr. Theodore Morgan, was supervising the operation. Dr. Morgan was much younger than the chief, well-spoken, well-dressed, and considered himself something of a 'ladies' man.' The chief disliked Dr. Morgan's know-it-all attitude. Just because he had this 'highfalutin' degree, he felt the doctor treated him no better than a gloried traffic cop.

Chief McGraw hurried over to Dr. Morgan and motioned to the site and asked, "What you think about this, Morgan?"

Dr. Morgan turned to him, smirked, and said, "Isn't that your department, McGraw? I'm just here to pick up the bones and perform the analysis."

"It's your job to figure out who it is!" retorted McGraw as he glared back at him and walked back to his car.

***

Addison Temple leaned back in her office chair and ran her fingers through her thick, auburn hair. She was tired, no doubt about it. That late-night stake-out had taken its toll on her. Following deadbeat husbands for suspicious wives was not a fun part of her job! And, she did love her job! Being the only female private detective in the city really had its advantages. It gave her such a sense of 'self,' of being a 'strong' woman, not just figuratively, but intellectually. She was her own boss, something she had always wanted to be. She wasn't going to be sucked into being the 'typical' woman, not her! She craved adventure and independence and no man was going to take that away from her. She rose and looked out onto the city. It was getting late in the afternoon and she could see people hurrying down the sidewalk, presumably on the way to their homes and families. She had to admit that sometimes she wished she had a husband and family to go home to, but then, she came to her senses.

Addison Temple was what one would consider a 'looker.' She was tall and well-built. Her green eyes and complexion were nothing short of enchanting. Her legs went on for miles, it seems. She believed in using her looks to her best advantage when it came to male clients. There had been a few male clients who had doubted her detective abilities but certainly had not doubted her 'female' abilities. However, after seeing the results of her work, they soon changed their minds on the first score. They had discovered that she was good at her job—something she already knew. It had taken a lot of hard work to get where she was today, and she was determined to stay there.

There was a knock at the door and she turned. In walked her trusted secretary, Stella Downey. Stella had been with her since the beginning. Often, Stella had gone without pay in those early days until the money had started coming in. Stella was not what you might call 'pretty' in the usual sense of the word, but she had something else—call it personality if you like. She could out wise-crack anyone, and usually did. Today, her dyed blonde hair swung against her shoulders as she swayed across the floor. "Boss, there is a young lady here to see you—she says it's important. Shall I say you are too busy right now and ask her to come back later? You look so tired," she said with a look of concern as she saw the look of fatigue on Addison's face.

Addison replied, "That's all right, Stella, I'm okay—just a late-night stake-out and you know how they can be!"

Stella nodded, and her dyed blond hair seemed to nod as well. She answered with a smile, "Maybe it won't take long, Boss. I just couldn't help but ask if you could see her—she looks so desperate. I'll show her in."

In a minute, she was being addressed by a young woman of about 25 or 30 years of age, "Miss Temple, my name is Ava Richardson." Addison shook hands with the woman and noticed the woman's hand was shaking and felt clammy.

"Please have a seat," said Addison as she pointed at the chair in front of her desk. "Can I get you anything, coffee perhaps?"

"No, no, thank you," was the woman's response.

"Well then, let's get down to the reason for your visit today," Addison stated. She looked across at the young woman seated in front of her with a smile.

Addison took note of the details of the woman's appearance and dress. Her hair was worn short with little fuss and her dress was simple. She wore little makeup. Her hands were strong, and it appeared she had done domestic work as her hands were a bit red and rough. A gold wedding ring could be seen on her left hand. Addison wondered why the woman was here and why she appeared so anxious.

Addison tried to put the woman at ease. "Please just tell me who you are and why you need my help," she said reassuringly.

Ava clasped her hands tightly in her lap and swallowed, "My name is Ava Richardson and I live on the edge of town. I am here because I need you to find my parents. I am adopted, you know, and have never known who they are."

Addison watched her client begin fidgeting with her purse, opening and closing the clasp nervously. "Why are you seeking the identities of your parents now, since I assume you were adopted at a very young age?" she asked.

"I need to learn more about my genetic history, you see, Ms. Temple. My doctor wants me to learn all I can to make recommendations for my son's treatment. He may die if I don't find out, and soon," replied Ava. Her voice had started to shake as tears welled up in her eyes.

Addison grabbed a tissue and handed it to the woman. She couldn't but be moved by what she saw. Ava blew her nose loudly and continued, "You see, Miss Temple, my son has been diagnosed with a rare genetic disease called ALD. ALD is a brain disorder, which can lead to death. If he receives treatment early enough, there is a chance he will live. That's why I must learn all I can about my genetic past."

Addison asked carefully, "How old were you when you were adopted and where are your adoptive parents now?"

"I was adopted right after I was born in the hospital, which was in Drayton, a few miles to the west of Glendale. My adoptive parents said they never knew who my birth parents had been and said the records had been sealed. They were both killed in a car accident over ten years ago," Ava managed to answer.

Addison asked, "What was the name of the hospital?"

"Drayton Community General Hospital; it's the only one in Drayton but they won't tell you anything—I already tried," answered Ava as she sniffed and blew her nose loudly.

Addison made some notes on a pad. "Are you married, Ms. Richardson?" She asked.

Ava answered with a wary look, "Yes, my husband's name is Samuel."

"Is there more than the one child?" asked Addison.

"I have two boys, three and six years old," was the response. "They are my biggest worry, Ms. Temple, and I need to learn more about my medical history for their sakes. I don't care about me!" said Ava as her voice caught in her throat.

"How does your husband feel about you finding your birth parents?" asked Addison while watching her visitor closely.

"He doesn't think it will do any good to try to look for them and doesn't want to waste the money," she answered with her eyes lowered. She started opening and clasping her purse once again, fingers shaking.

Addison put down her pen and shook her auburn hair out of her eyes. Her expression was thoughtful. This woman was no doubt in a desperate situation and needed her help badly. If there was one thing Addison knew, it was a desperate client, and she had one in front of her now. Obviously, the woman did not have a lot of money and would have to deal with her 'jerk' of a husband about the bill for her services. "Mrs. Richardson, based on what you have told me so far, it sounds like you really need help finding your parents, but are worried about the cost to do so?" she asked quietly.

Ava shook her head affirmatively and said, "Yes, Miss Temple, that's exactly it," as her eyes once again lowered to her lap.

Addison reached for the intercom, buzzed Stella, and said, "Stella, Mrs. Richardson will be coming out in a few minutes to give you her address and other details. We will be giving her case top priority. Get a hold of Farley as soon as you can and have him give me a call. I know he's on a case out of town, but it's urgent that I speak with him today if possible."

Addison explained to Mrs. Richardson, "Farley is my associate and my right-hand around here."

"Okay, Boss, right away," Stella answered, and Addison replaced the receiver.

"But, how much will this cost?" Ava asked worriedly. "Can I pay in installments?" she added.

Addison smiled assuredly and replied, "Don't worry about that right now, we will work something out."

Ava's worried expression changed to one of hope. "I am so glad I came to see you, Miss Temple," she said. "You have given me new hope," she added.

Addison shook hands with her new client and showed her to the door. As she shut it, Addison had a vaguely uneasy feeling. She walked to her desk and reached for her phone. Before she could begin dialing, however, her door opened and there stood her mother. Addison felt her heart sink and thought to herself, *oh no, here we go again, she's got that "motherly" look again!*

Addison's mother, Olivia Temple, was truly what one would call a "throwback" to the fifties. Picture Donna Reed on steroids and you have just described Olivia Temple. Today, she was fresh from the beauty parlor. Her just-cut bobbed hair showed off blonde highlights to perfection. Olivia was young-looking for her age—she, of course, denied being over 40 to anyone who had the audacity to even hint she was closer to 50. Addison's father, Stanley Temple, had died of a gunshot wound he received during what was supposed to have been a routine police investigation ten years ago. It had devastated both Olivia and Addison. Being an only child, Addison had worshipped her father and they had done everything together. Addison got her love for the world of the private detective from her father who had been the chief of police before Carter McGraw took over. Olivia Temple had adored her husband and wanted the same type of marriage for her daughter, much to Addison's dismay a lot of the time. A husband is not what Addison had in mind for herself—at least not right now. Olivia had made it her mission in life to change all of that and took it upon herself to arrange dates for Addison routinely. In the last month, Addison had literally been introduced to a minimum of a dozen men, all of whom were hand-picked by her mother.

Olivia swirled into the office with a look of a tigress on the prowl for game. "Darling, you look so tired, have you been getting enough sleep?" she asked while hugging her daughter.

Addison endured the embrace and waited for her mother to begin. And she was absolutely correct. Olivia launched into her "Why don't you find a nice young man and forget all this detective nonsense" speech. How many times had she heard this? Hundreds, no, thousands of times.

Addison waited and finally, just as her mother was pausing for breath, Addison interrupted, "Mother, for the thousandth time, I enjoy what I do and somehow, when I do this work, I feel closer to Dad. You can understand that, can't you?"

Addison knew how to handle her mother. Just the mention of her husband always brought Olivia back to safe ground. "I suppose you are right. You know how much we all miss him. Not a day goes by that I don't want him back by my side. Have you been out with your friends lately? Anyone special that I should know about?" Olivia asked, still trying to keep the interrogation going.

Addison smiled lovingly at her mother and shook her head, "No, mother, I have really been swamped here the last couple of weeks; but, don't worry, I'll find some free time soon and I promise to get out there and socialize!"

Olivia looked at her only child and thought, *she is so lovely and would make some lucky man such a good wife*, but instead said, "I do hope so, Addison, because you must know I only want what is best for you."

Just then, the intercom buzzed and Stella's voice sounded, "Boss, Farley is on the phone."

"Thanks, Stella, I'll take it," replied Addison. "Mother, I am sorry, but I really need to take this call. It has to do with a new client."

"Oh, all right, dear, but I will be expecting you for dinner at the end of the week," Olivia announced as she managed to gain a reverse swirling momentum out of the office door.

Chapter 2

Logan Stanton walked into the Glendale Police Department and greeted the desk sergeant, "Hello Jack, how's it going?"

Jack Walters looked up from his computer and grunted, "How do you think it's going, Stanton, working on this blame machine?" Jack Walters, a desk sergeant for over 20 years, hated two things in this world with a passion—his bunions and computers!

Logan smiled with a nod and asked, "Computer giving you trouble again, Jack? Can I help?"

"Do you think I'd take help from some private dick? Besides, the chief would have my badge; this stuff is confidential!" answered Walters as he plucked away even harder on the keyboard as if pressing with more force would be the answer to his troubles.

Logan's smile turned into a grin and he asked, "Speaking of the chief, is he in?"

The desk sergeant glared at his keyboard and managed to ask, "Got an appointment?"

Logan's grin broadened and he said, "Sure thing, the 'big guy' called me himself this morning and wanted me to come right over. I'd tell you what it's about but it's 'confidential'."

Jack's head shot up, "Are you trying to get smart with me, Stanton?"

"Who, me? I wouldn't dream of it, Sarge," as Logan's grin grew.

The sergeant grabbed the phone and growled, "Chief, it's that Stanton dick to see you. OK Chief, I'll tell him."

"You know where it is," said Sergeant Walters looking back down at his keyboard.

"Gee, thanks so much, Jack, always so great to see you," replied Logan as he saluted and turned to walk down the hall to Chief McGraw's office. He knocked on the door and stepped inside.

Chief McGraw looked up from his desk and took stock of the man in front of him. Logan Stanton was just too damn good-looking for his own good. No man should be that good-looking. He watched him walk toward him and couldn't help but admire the way he moved. He walked with a cat-like grace and anyone watching him could not but notice the broad, muscular physique and the chiseled features of his face. He was a tall man—at least six-foot-three. His hair was dark, and his eyes were a distinctive light blue. It was a face that smiled readily and often. He knew that although Logan smiled a lot, his smile could vanish just as easily. Unfortunately, there had been many criminals who had learned that fact about Logan the hard way. Chief McGraw mentally shook his mind clear of his thoughts and extended his hand. Logan shook it firmly. Chief McGraw noticed the firmness and liked it.

"Hello, Chief, always good to see you. Why did you want to see me?" asked Logan, smiling.

Chief McGraw cleared his throat and said, "Stanton, it's this case on the body found under the Catholic Church bell tower."

"What about it?" asked Logan with an inquiring look. "I thought you had that case pretty well buttoned up already."

"That's just the trouble—we have run into a couple of snags," said Chief McGraw, nervously shuffling through a file on his desk while avoiding Logan's eyes.

"What sort of snags, Chief?" asked Logan.

"Well, for one thing, although the forensic guys have managed to figure out the body is a male, about 35–40 years of age, they haven't got much to go on since they figure he was buried when the tower was built about 30 years ago," the chief explained reluctantly.

"But, surely, in this day and age of investigations, the fact that the body had been buried so long ago shouldn't be a problem," replied Logan.

"Well, it turns out it's more of a problem than we originally thought and so that's why I called you," Chief McGraw explained with some trepidation.

"You know I will help in any way that I can, Chief, but, first, why don't you tell me what this is really all about?" Logan said, flashing one of his bigger-than-usual smiles.

"Oh, all right Stanton, I should have known I couldn't slide one past you," McGraw replied grudgingly. "You see, the commissioner is getting on me to solve the case and I have no leads and I could use some help—just because our department is so short of manpower, you understand. Why, if we had more officers, we would have this case solved in a couple of days," McGraw added while trying not to look worried.

Logan just kept on smiling in his usual charming way, which he knew had the nasty effect of irritating the chief. "Why, Chief, are you actually saying you need my help on this one?" he went on to say.

"Yes, damn you, Stanton, yes!" answered McGraw trying to keep the snarl out of his voice.

"Chief, I am truly honored and accept gladly," replied Logan with a smile that spoke volumes.

"Fine then, go over to forensics and get what we have so far on the case—they're expecting you," said McGraw, trying to avoid eye contact.

"You must have been pretty sure that I would say yes, Chief," Logan looked amused as he got up from the chair across from McGraw's desk.

Chief McGraw pretended not to hear him and started busily shuffling the papers on his desk.

***

Addison picked up the phone and greeted her right-hand man, Farley Brooks. "Hello, Farley, how are things going?" Farley had been with her agency since the beginning. He was good at what he did, and she knew it. He had become a father figure to her since the death of her father. Farley was getting on in years, but he was in no way letting that insignificant detail slow him down. He was in better shape than a lot of guys who were half his age and he made sure he did everything he could to stay that way. She called him the 'Silver Fox' for a couple of reasons—his wavy silver hair and his savviness when it came to detective work. Addison often wondered if he wasn't just more than a little bit interested in her mother, but she thought it best not to pry—at least not now.

"What's up?" Farley's familiar voice came over the phone.

"A new client—a woman looking for her birth parents—showed up in the office a bit ago," replied Addison.

"That's not our usual type of case, is it?" questioned Farley.

"You're right, it isn't, but, after talking with her and hearing her story, I couldn't help myself," replied Addison.

"Well, whatever you think—you're the boss," was Farley's reply. "What do you want me to do?" was his next question.

"I know you are on a case near Drayton and since the client says she was born at the hospital there, I'd like you to find out anything you can on the woman's adoption and, hopefully, any information leading to the identities of her birth parents," replied Addison and then suggested she transfer his call to Stella who would fill him in on the details of the case.

"I'll be in touch as soon as I have something to report," Farley assured her,

"It might not be easy, but if anyone can do it, you can!" Addison replied and promptly transferred him to Stella's phone.

***

Addison Temple walked into the Glendale Police Department's training facility and heads turned—they usually did when she walked in—not only because she was a woman, since there were not many women who used the facility, but still fewer women who looked like Addison Temple looked. Today, she looked particularly noticeable since she had on leather pants that did a great deal to enhance her natural endowments. Addison didn't notice, or if she did, didn't really care to notice; she had other things on her mind, like pistol practice. She took advantage of the police department's practice facility to brush up on her skills whenever she had some time and today was it.

As one might expect, Addison really didn't need much brushing up—her aim was dead-on and soon, she had several members of Glendale's finest watching her shoot. In a pause while new targets were being set up, a voice said quietly behind her, "How about a contest, just you and me?" Addison stopped loading her gun and a small smile came over her face and something stirred within her, which she quickly suppressed; after all the voice was just another voice. Who was she kidding? It was his voice all right—that irritating, arrogant, smiling individual who always seemed to know exactly which buttons to push where she was concerned.

Addison turned and there he was, all smiles, of course. She silently caught her breath as she took in his virile good looks and sheer masculinity—it always had the same effect on her, somehow leaving her breathless and slightly unsettled. She was quick to hide her reactions and responded, "Why if it isn't Glendale's foremost male private detective! You do notice, I said 'male' detective."

"You flatter me, my dear Miss Temple," Logan Stanton's smile broadened. His eyes traveled down her body, taking in every curve. "You look positively alluring today," he continued.

Addison's green eyes turned into molten emeralds and her cheeks flushed—how dare he look at her that way! The insolent Neanderthal! To cover her confusion, she snapped back, "Mr. Stanton, if you are finished observing the scenery, I am ready to take you up on your challenge."

"With pleasure, Miss Temple, to be sure," was his smiling reply.

They both took their places in front of their respective targets. 'Ladies first,' Logan gave a small bow. Addison glared and took aim. Although she shot well, somehow, each of her shots was just slightly off the bullseye. She blamed it on the audience watching—it had grown considerably and there just were too many spectators! Who was she kidding? She knew it wasn't the spectators that were disturbing her concentration; it was that damn man! Logan's aim, on the other hand, was true and each shot managed to be right on target—bullseye each time.

"Miss Temple, your aim seems to be a bit off today. Anything the matter? Can I be of service?" he gave her one of his most innocent smiles.

"There is absolutely nothing wrong, Mr. Stanton. Thank you for the target practice, but I must be going. You see, unlike some people, I have work to do on a very important new case. Good day!" Addison managed to grind out before grabbing her things and walking quickly out of the door.

Laughter followed her like the last few strains of a haunting ballad before the door slammed behind her.

Chapter 3

Logan Stanton laughed out loud as he drove downtown to meet with the forensics guys. Thinking about Addison was a favorite pastime and he wouldn't admit to anyone just how often he did think about her. She was like no other woman he had known—and there had been a few! A man like Logan was someone who enjoyed the company of women and who had no trouble finding able and willing women to accommodate him. What was it about Addison that intrigued him so much, he thought as he turned the corner onto Belmont Street on which the big brick City Police/Government building was located. She was perhaps the best-looking woman he had ever seen, but yet that wasn't it—he had known a lot of beautiful women. No, there was something about her that was truly undefinable, something so different that he really couldn't put a finger on it. He kept on trying, though, but each time, failing miserably. He knew one thing for sure, though, and that was that she got under his skin and he wanted to scratch that itch terribly!

Logan got out of his brand-new sports car—how he loved driving fast cars—and lovingly gave it one last look before walking up the steps into the building. He had shopped a very long time before finally deciding on a Dodge Challenger. It was a black metallic with a black interior. He had a customized exhaust system installed for improved performance. He enjoyed his 'toy' and took it out for a 'spin' whenever he could. Heads turned when they saw it go by, of course; it was unknown if they turned due to the car or due to its driver—at least, on the part of the women!

He stopped at the information desk and told the pretty receptionist that he was expected by Dr. Morgan. The smile she gave him was clearly an invitation, so he gave her one of his "I like what I see" smiles but left it at that. He strode down the hall and opened the door marked "Lab" and walked in.

Dr. Theodore Morgan looked up from the cadaver he was working on and grimaced, "Oh, it's you, Stanton. McGraw warned me you would be stopping by."

"How're things, Doc?" asked Logan, smiling as usual. The doctor always amused Logan. Today, he was impeccably groomed and was wearing an obviously expensive pair of suit pants and shirt underneath his blood-speckled lab coat. Logan always got the feeling when he saw Dr. Morgan that he was a man in need of a gift subscription to an online dating service; in other words, he needed to find a woman and needed to update his methods of doing so.

"So, can you fill me in on what you have so far on the body found under the church bell tower?" asked Logan, while trying not to look at the cadaver's stomach contents.

"Give me a couple of minutes to clean up and we will talk in my office," answered Dr. Morgan after looking up just in time to see Logan's face turn a peculiar green color.

"Thanks, Doc, I'll just step in your office right now," as Logan turned to open the doctor's office door with some relief.

Dr. Morgan strode in a few minutes later, looking dapper in his custom-made suit and Italian leather shoes. Logan couldn't resist teasing him. "Hot date after work tonight, Doc?" he asked with a big smile.

"That would be none of your business, Stanton," was the curt reply. "You stick to your social life and I will stick to mine," he added, looking irritated.

"Just asking, Doc, because you look like you came straight out of a men's fashion magazine," Logan remarked with a twinkle in his eye.

"Let's get down to business, shall we?" Dr. Morgan said as he opened the manila file on his desk. "The tests conducted on the remains found beneath the tower indicate that the body had been there about 25–30 years, judging by its condition. The body is a male, about 30–35 years of age, give or take, of medium height and size. Death had occurred due to a blow to the skull, most likely caused by a 'blunt' instrument. The only recognizable effect found near the body was this cross," as Dr. Morgan pulled a rather tarnished, dirty cross out of the file folder.

"That's about all we have been able to determine thus far from the evidence obtained from the scene," added Dr. Morgan, sounding a bit bored with it all. "We really haven't the time to spend trying to dig into a 30-year-old murder case, Stanton," he pointed out in a rather defensive voice.

"Well, Doc, aren't you lucky that I'm here and that I do have the time?" replied Logan with yet another smile, making sure to focus it squarely toward Dr. Morgan.

***

Farley Brooks was getting frustrated and when Farley Brooks got frustrated, everyone knew about it. This time, the people who had the misfortune to be visiting the Drayton Community General Hospital that day and who were within hearing distance of Farley Brooks were made aware of that frustration. "All I want is the name of the agency that handled the adoption," could be heard down the hall from the business office of the hospital, "and nothing more."

"Mr. Brooks, you must understand that adoption records are sealed, and we cannot divulge this information," Mrs. Samuels, the business manager, said, trying to remain calm but not achieving her goal.

"Look, lady, the name of the adoption agency is not part of the sealed records. I will deal with them directly with any questions that I may have," spat out Farley.

Mrs. Samuels looked like she might faint at any moment, turning first red, then pale. "If you will excuse me, Mr. Brooks, I will need to speak to the hospital administrator, Mr. Adams, about your request," Mrs. Samuels managed to get out.

"You do that and make it snappy!" growled Farley while pacing up and down in front of her desk.

***

Addison drove all the way back to her office and was very fortunate that she had left many of Glendale's finest at the training center because she probably broke every speed limit set by that department along the route. That infuriating, arrogant man! How dare he behave the way he does—always trying to irritate her and visibly enjoying it when he knows he was successful, which is most of the time! She came to a stop in the parking lot with a screech and got out. She made a quick assessment to make sure no one would be able to park too close to her baby—a sports car she had worked so hard for and one that she and the bank had a mutual interest in—she loved her car and protected it at all costs, even it meant walking further than necessary just to ensure a safe parking spot. Little did she realize it, but she and her nemesis had more in common than she knew!

Addison dashed in the agency door, greeting Stella as she raced by her desk. "How's it going?" she tossed at her on the way past.

Stella looked up, blinked, and then watched her boss sail by. There was only one person who could have such an effect on her boss and that person was none other than Logan Stanton! Stella stood up and followed Addison to her office and shut the door behind her. "So, where did you see Mr. Stanton?" she asked as innocently as she could, given the circumstances.

"What makes you think I saw Logan Stanton?" asked Addison while looking for some telltale sign of laughter in the secretary's face.

"From my experience, he is the only person who could turn you into such a 'hot mess,' Boss!" replied Stella while trying to keep the smile off her face.

"Oh, all right, I did happen to run into him at the police training center, if you must know!" admitted Addison reluctantly.

"I see, and how was the hunkiest detective this side of the Mason-Dixon Line?" asked Stella, getting a dreamy look on her face.

"Stella, might I remind you that we run a professional agency and we have no time for anything other than serving our clients!" Addison said with a disapproving look.

The dreamy look did not fade, however, as Stella remarked, "I'd be glad to serve Logan Stanton anytime!"

Chapter 4

Farley Brooks walked into Addison's office and slumped into a chair. Addison looked up from her computer and saw the 'Silver Fox' looking somewhat less than his usual confident self. "Boss, I've had a tough time finding information on this adoption case. I just got back from Drayton and let me tell you, it's like pulling teeth!" said Farley with a yawn he tried his best to suppress.

Addison noticed for the first time how tired he looked. Her 'Silver Fox' was beginning to show a few signs of age, especially as he sat in the morning sunshine coming in her office window. Maybe he needed to slow down a bit; she must talk to him about that, but not now—later would be better.

"What did you manage to learn?" asked Addison while pouring a cup of coffee and handing it over to him.

Farley nodded his thanks and said, "I finally got the name of the adoption agency that handled the case. I contacted them, and they gave me some general information only. The adoption took place immediately after the child was born and took place at the hospital. The adoptive parents were in their late thirties, Caucasian, and both were high school graduates. The child was placed for adoption because the mother was unmarried at the time and did not feel she could care for the child. The birth mother had no other children at the time. That's about all I could find out without a court order." Farley looked disappointed.

"Good work, Farley; don't worry, we'll get more information," assured Addison.

"How do you plan to do that?" asked Farley as he drained his cup.

"Because the adoptee needs to know who her birth parents are for medical reasons, the judge should grant a court order to have the adoption records unsealed. I will call him tomorrow and make an appointment to see him," replied Addison in a confident voice.

"I sure hope you're right, Boss!" replied Farley as he walked out of the door.

***

Logan Stanton spent most of the morning at the public library. It was a place he was not all that familiar with since he hadn't spent a lot of time there in the past. Logan just wasn't a 'literary' type of guy. He was too busy solving cases and being chased by women to ever be interested in books. Today, he was there because he thought it might be the best place to start trying to dig into what was happening in Glendale about 25–30 years ago.

He had poured over the past issues of the Glendale Gazette going back two decades and was still working on the third decade. His head hurt, and he was sure his eyes were starting to cross. If it hadn't been for the cute librarian bringing him coffee every hour, he would have nodded off hours ago. He was going to give it one more hour and if he still hadn't run across anything that could possibly help solve the case of the dead body found under the tower, he was going to hang it up! Logan clicked on the next issue on the library website and started paging through. He was just thinking that it really was amazing how advertising had changed over the years when his eye caught a story on a missing person on page two. It read: "Father Sebastian Antonio, priest of Our Lady of the Lake Catholic Church for the past two years, is believed to be missing. Father Sebastian had left town a month ago to attend a retreat at the Our Lady of the Saints monastery located in Mount Scranton. According to Father Tobias of the monastery, Father Sebastian never arrived. An investigation is currently underway to determine Father Sebastian's whereabouts."

Suddenly, Logan's mind flashed back to the dirty, tarnished cross found next to the body. He jumped up and shouted "Yes!" before he realized what he had done. The head librarian—incidentally, not as cute as the other one— looked disapprovingly at him and 'shushed' him severely. Logan winked at her and gave her one of his most charming smiles, which was guaranteed to thaw even the most disapproving librarian around!

***

Addison pressed the intercom and asked, "Stella, would you get Judge Talbot on the line for me?"

"Sure thing, Boss, right away. If he's busy, shall I leave a message to call you?" replied Stella.

"Yes, make sure the message says it's urgent that I speak with him," answered Addison.

Stella buzzed a couple of minutes later and announced, "The judge is on the line for you, Boss."

"Thanks, Stella," Addison replied as she reached for her phone.

"Hello, Judge, how are you?" Addison asked.

"Just fine, Addison, how's my favorite detective in the world?" replied Judge Talbot. Judge Talbot had been a close friend of Addison's father for years prior to the death of Mr. Temple and remained close to Addison and her mother.

"I'm also fine, Judge, it's been a while since we talked," said Addison with real affection in her voice.

"Most definitely, it has been way too long. What can I do for you, Addison?" asked the judge.

Addison proceeded to explain about Ava Richardson, her adoption, and the sealed records. After giving a quick summary, Addison informed Judge Talbot of Ava's need for information regarding her genetic history and why the adoption records must be unsealed as soon as possible. "In other words, you need me to draw up a court order that will unseal the records?" asked Judge Talbot.

"You got it, Judge, would you willing to do that for me?" asked Addison with a smile that showed through the phone.

"Yes, of course, I will. You know I am always ready to help in any way I can!" replied the Judge with genuine affection in his tone. "I will have it for you tomorrow morning. Would that be OK?" continued Judge Talbot.

"Of course, Judge, you are the sweetest!" answered Addison. "Please give my love to your wife," Addison added.

"Sure thing, Addison—you know if I were 20 years younger and not married to the 'love of my life,' I believe I would be standing on your doorstep!" replied Judge Talbot.

Addison chuckled as she hung up the phone. Nothing to do now but wait for tomorrow!

***

The judge was as good as his word because promptly the next morning, Addison had the court order to unseal Ava Richardson's adoption records on her desk. She phoned Farley Brooks at his home. Farley was taking a couple of days off after being on cases non-stop for two weeks. "Farley, sorry to bother you at home, but I did manage to get the court order from Judge Talbot and since you are already familiar with the adoption agency, would you mind driving back to Drayton and presenting it to them?" asked Addison.

"You bet, Boss, I'm anxious to button this up. I'll be in to pick it up in an hour," replied Farley, his voice showing his pleasure that Addison had been successful in obtaining it.

"Thanks, Farley, I knew you would!" was Addison's reply.

***

Grace Evans stood looking out of her picture window and wondered who the woman was who had just pulled up in a bright red sports car in front of her house in Glendale. She had never seen her before. As the woman got out of her car, Grace could see she was tall, well-dressed, and very attractive. The one thing that caught her eye more than anything was the way she walked, with grace and confidence. *Oh well, the woman must be selling something or has the wrong house.* Grace went to the door when the doorbell rang and said, "Yes, what is it?"

Addison Temple's experience as a detective had taught her to assess most people in just a few seconds. She saw a woman of perhaps 50 years old or so with dyed blonde hair who was apparently trying to look younger than she really was, judging by the amount of makeup she was wearing. Addison also noted the dress the woman was wearing—a bit too revealing and a bit too tight since it showed off her extra rolls to perfection. Addison smiled and asked, "Are you Grace Evans?"

"Who's asking?" replied Grace.

"My name is Addison Temple," replied Addison handing Grace her card.

"You're a private detective? What do you want?" asked Grace, her face appearing even more sullen.

"Before I get into the reason for my being here, are you Grace Evans?" insisted Addison.

After some hesitation, Grace said, "Yes. I'm Grace Evans; what's it to you?"

Addison kept on smiling and asked politely, "May I come in, so we can talk privately?"

Grace Evans stood looking at her with a wary look on her face and thought hard. What could this woman want with her? Why was she here? She didn't like being bothered by strangers; she minded her own business and she liked it that way! As the seconds silently ticked by, Grace finally stepped back from the doorway and Addison walked in.

"Well?" asked Grace.

"May I sit down?" Addison asked pointing at the sofa.

Grace nodded and lead the way into the room. They both sat down, and Addison pulled out a file from her briefcase. Addison opened the file and said, "Ms. Evans, a client of mine hired me to locate you and that's why I'm here."

Grace Evans visibly took a breath and asked cautiously, "Oh? Who could that be?"

"My client claims to be your daughter, Ms. Evans," Addison said while carefully watching for a reaction. She was not disappointed. Grace Evans's face turned ashen and her hands visibly shook.

"There must be some mistake. I have no children," she managed to get out.

"Are you sure about that?" asked Addison with some amazement. Grace Evans stood up and walked to the picture window once again and looked out onto the street. She stood that way for several minutes until Addison finally asked, "Is everything all right, Ms. Evans? I know this must have come as quite a shock to you."

Grace Evans finally turned from the window and stared at Addison. "She says she is my daughter? How do you know she isn't lying?" asked Grace, trying not to show her nervousness. "I told you I have no children, remember?"

Addison handed Grace the file and said, "Please have a look at this, Ms. Evans, I have a feeling you may change your mind."

Chapter 5

Grace Evans's hands shook as she reached for the file. Addison noticed the fear in her eyes. *Why was she so afraid?* She could understand there might be anxiety, but why fear? *Wouldn't someone in her position be just a little bit excited to learn she may have just found a long-lost daughter? Something was not quite right here.*

Grace read silently for some time and finally put the file down and looked at Addison. She said nothing. Addison stared back and finally said, "Well, Ms. Evans, what do you think now?"

Grace spoke slowly and rather softly, "I guess I have a daughter."

Addison was astonished by the woman's reaction but hid it. "Can you tell me about what the circumstances were that resulted in the adoption?" she asked.

Grace looked worried. "What's there to talk about? I got pregnant and that was that."

"I certainly respect your privacy, but my client is also interested in learning more about her father as well. Can you tell me who he is?" Addison said firmly.

"No, I will not and cannot tell you who her father was," said Grace and looked away.

"Do you mean you were involved with more than one man at the time, or that you simply won't share that information?" asked Addison.

"It isn't anyone's business but mine," responded Grace with an edge in her voice that was unmistakable.

"What about your daughter? Isn't it her business too?" responded Addison with equal firmness.

Grace didn't say a thing for a couple of minutes. Then she said, "The only person that I will tell that to would be my daughter and no one else."

Addison's first thought was, *What is this woman hiding from me and from the rest of the world and why is she using the past tense referring to the father?* Instead, she asked, "Does that mean you are willing to meet your daughter?"

Grace fumbled with the file and finally, handed it back to Addison, and replied, "All right, I'll meet her, but, only if we meet alone without anyone else, including you!"

Addison nodded and asked, "When and where do you want to meet with her?"

Grace answered with little emotion, "The sooner, the better, but I don't want to meet her at my home; it's got to be somewhere else."

***

Logan Stanton sped along the state highway as fast as he dared in his black sedan. It was over two hours' drive to the Our Lady of the Saints monastery in Mount Scranton and he didn't want to waste any time getting there. What he didn't need was another speeding ticket!

He finally reached his destination and drove up the driveway to the rather imposing building. As he parked and walked up the steps, he noticed the innate peace that the entire building seemed to emit. There seemed to be a feeling of 'serenity' that hit him as soon as he walked inside. The walls were decorated with paintings of various saints and other religious artifacts while the ceiling of the entrance was made of beautiful stained glass. Logan Stanton was welcomed by a priest who led him to the office of Father Andrew, head of the order.

"It is a pleasure to welcome you to our monastery, Mr. Stanton," said Father Andrew as he indicated a chair for Logan. The hand Father Andrew offered to Logan as he sat down was old and wrinkled, as was Father Andrew, but yet, somehow, the elderly priest still appeared to exhibit some degree of youthfulness.

"Thank you, Father, I appreciate you're taking the time to talk with me," replied Logan.

"You said on the phone that you have some questions about a murder case you are working on," asked Father Andrew as he seated himself behind the huge oak desk.

"Yes, I do. I am working on a murder that took place about 30 years ago. The body had been buried under the Catholic Church bell tower in Glendale, where I live. I was called in on the case by the Glendale Chief of Police to give him a hand," explained Logan.

"Have you been able to discover any information about the dead body thus far, Mr. Stanton?" asked Father Andrew as he leaned back in his chair.

Logan leaned forward and said excitedly, "Yes, sir, I have."

"I suspected you must have learned something because you made the trip to see us," smiled Father Andrew and continued, "Please tell me so that I can help, if I can."

"I did some research at our public library and discovered a newspaper article from nearly 30 years ago about a priest who had left Glendale to attend a retreat at this monastery and who had never returned," responded Logan. Logan went on to provide details about Father Sebastian Antonio including the fact he had only been serving the Our Lady of the Lake Catholic Church in Glendale for about two years as well as the cross that was found near the body.

"And you are here to find out if Father Sebastian Antonio ever attended the retreat all those years ago. Am I correct?" asked Father Andrew.

Logan nodded excitedly and said, "Yes, Father, that is exactly why I am here."

"I will be glad to check our records. You must understand that was a very long time ago and we were not computerized back then. A manual search must be conducted," cautioned the Father with a smile.

"I understand, Father and I appreciate anything you can do for me," assured Logan.

Father Andrew stood up and shook Logan's hand and said, "Please give us a day or so. Are you staying in town?"

"Yes, at the Hotel Scranton. I can be reached there," replied Logan as he stood up.

"I will call you as soon as I learn any information," said Father Andrew as he walked Logan to the door.

Chapter 6

Addison walked into her office looking rather tired once again. Stella watched her cross over to her private office and shook her head disapprovingly. She not only thought Addison was a great boss but a great person. Sometimes, however, her boss just needed to take time for herself. She needed to realize there is more in life than her work. She needed a man in her life! Stella knew exactly who that man should be. Too bad, her boss didn't know! Her thoughts were interrupted by the buzzing of the intercom. "Yes, Boss?" asked Stella.

"Would you call Ava Richardson and ask her to come to see me as soon as possible?" asked Addison.

"Right away, Boss!" responded Stella.

***

Ava Richardson walked into Addison's private office with a look of anticipation on her face. Addison looked up and smiled. "How are you today, Ava?" she asked.

Ava didn't smile as she sat down in the chair across from Addison. "I'm doing OK, do you have any news for me?" was all she said.

Addison watched her client shift nervously in her chair and noticed how Ava's hands shook as they unclasped and clasped in her lap. Addison could understand how Ava might be somewhat anxious about any news that was coming her way, but she could not understand why Ava was so obviously nervous. This fact bothered Addison, although she couldn't put her finger on it nor could she understand exactly why it should.

Addison picked up the file on her desk and opened it slowly. "Ava, we located your birth mother," was all she said and carefully watched for the reaction. The reaction came immediately. In the split second that Ava first heard the news, Addison thought she saw a glimpse of excitement that was just as quickly gone, masked by a look of intense relief and thankfulness, which made Addison unsure about what she had seen in that split second and indeed if it had actually been there or not.

Ava reached for her bag and took out a tissue, "Ms. Temple, you just don't know how that makes me feel!" she said as she dried her eyes.

"I have been waiting for this moment for so long!" Ava whispered softly. "I just can't believe it's really true!"

Addison described the meeting with Ava's mother, Grace Evans, in detail, including the part about the lack of information about her birth father, to Ava. Ava listened carefully to every word without a trace of nervousness—it had disappeared. Addison couldn't figure it out. What had made the change in Ava's demeanor? It bothered her, but she passed it off as a reaction to the shock of finding her mother.

"Your mother has consented to meet with you, Ava, if you are willing to do so," Addison said as she watched Ava closely. "Will you meet with her?" she continued.

Ava looked away from Addison's watchful gaze and said softly, "I'm willing since she is."

Addison hesitated for just a moment and then reached for the phone.

***

Logan Stanton lay on his hotel bed and stared at the ceiling. He noticed the cracks in the plaster. Someone had tried to cover them up with white paint, but not too successfully. His mind switched gears—it had a habit of doing that and often without advanced warning. He couldn't help smiling. He adored auburn hair and pairing it with green eyes was simply fascinating! He had never met a woman like Addison Temple and something inside of him told him that he probably never would! Everything about her intrigued him. There was no denying how beautiful she was and that was what had held his attention at first. Looks like hers were not easy to forget. And, he was a man after all. However, it went beyond the physical attraction, which was something unusual for him. He loved women and knew they loved him. All he had to do was look in the mirror to know why—he was good-looking, no doubt about it. It was different somehow with Addison, though. She didn't seem to notice, or if she did, she hid it well. She appeared oblivious to his looks as well as his masculinity, of which there was plenty. He had thought at first that it was the fact that she ignored these admirable qualities about him that had attracted him. But he knew it was more, so much more. She was smart, and what's more, she was a damn good detective. Besides, she had 'sass,' and 'class,' which are two things a lot of women do not possess from his extensive experience with the opposite sex.

The phone on the nightstand interrupted his thoughts with its shrill ring. He reached over and picked up the receiver. "Hello," said Logan with unintended briskness at being interrupted in his musings.

"I hope I am not disturbing you," said Father Andrew, "but you did ask me to call you with any information that I found on Father Sebastian."

"Oh, hello Father Andrew. I'm sorry if I was rather abrupt, but I was just taking a nap," Logan lied.

"No problem at all, Mr. Stanton," replied Father Andrew.

"Did you find anything on Father Sebastian's visit to your monastery all those years ago?" Logan asked, feeling a sense of excitement stirring inside of him.

"Yes, actually, I was able to learn something after some research of our old files," was Father Andrew's response.

"What did you find out?" asked Logan while trying to keep his voice calm.

"Well, our files were not kept up as efficiently as they are now due to computers; however, I did manage to discover that Father Sebastian had registered to attend a retreat a couple of weeks prior to the time of his alleged disappearance all those years ago," replied Father Andrew. "However, he never attended."

"That piece of information is helpful as it tells us that Father Sebastian had every intention of attending the retreat as scheduled," said Logan excitedly. "Was there anything else that you were able to learn about Father Sebastian?" he asked.

"Actually, yes, since the application for the retreat required the attendees to disclose information about their credentials," responded Father Andrew. "The application provides information regarding the seminary he attended as well as his priesthood appointments," he continued.

"Fantastic news," said Logan as he leaped off his bed. "May I have a copy made of the application?" he asked, nearly shouting.

"Of course, my dear boy, of course," replied Father Andrew while trying to keep his own voice calm. He hadn't ever been involved in a murder investigation before and couldn't help getting just a little excited himself!

"I'll be right there, Father!" said Logan as he hung up without waiting for Father Andrew's good-bye.

***

Addison replaced the phone receiver and turned to Ava. "Your mother will meet you but, she prefers to meet you somewhere other than at her house. I am sure you realize how this is pretty normal in situations like this one," assured Addison with careful attention to Ava's reaction.

But Ava showed no indication that she was upset by the request. She merely nodded her head and looked straight ahead. "Ms. Evans wishes to meet with you in Ames Park later tonight and suggested 8 o'clock at the bench near the fountain," stated Addison as matter-of-factly as she could.

Ava nodded again and rose from her chair. "Thank you, Ms. Temple," was all she said and walked out of the door, letting it slam shut behind her.

Chapter 7

Chief McGraw stood looking out of his window. He found it a fascinating pastime. He enjoyed watching the passers-by and wondered where they were going. Some walked purposefully, not even looking at others. Others strolled leisurely, taking in the day. Still, others would stop to chat and visit with those they knew along the way. People were so different, he thought, and so hard to figure. In all his years in law enforcement, they never ceased to amaze him. Maybe that is what kept him going in this thankless job! *Oh well, it will be all over soon.* Just a few months to go and he would retire. He could feel the fishing rod in his hand and see the sun shining on Lake Alcott already. His thoughts were interrupted by the abrupt opening of his office door.

Chief McGraw turned around and frowned. *There goes the daydream and back to reality, it was that damn smart-aleck detective again.* He bothered him, but he could never put a finger on why. Maybe it was his good looks, or maybe it was his arrogance. Either way, the irritation was there!

Logan Stanton threw himself into the chair across from the chief's desk and smiled. Chief McGraw grunted, "Good morning, Stanton, what do you want?"

"Why Chief, is that any way to speak to someone working on your side?" Logan asked and smiled even broader.

"What do mean, working on my side? You don't work for the Glendale Police, do you?" replied Chief McGraw. "Or do you know something that I don't?" Chief McGraw sat in his chair across from Logan and started shuffling through the papers on his desk in an attempt to look busy.

Logan watched him shuffle and chuckled, "Looking for something, Chief?"

Chief McGraw looked up and growled, "Only a place for you to go!"

Logan broke out into an actual guffaw this time and managed to say, "Chief, your sense of humor is improving by leaps and bounds!" He paused for breath. "Stop it, please!" Logan added when he finally caught his breath. "I can't take it anymore!"

"Why are you here, may I ask?" Chief McGraw nearly threw the papers across the desk. Somehow, he managed to control the impulse.

"Why, to give you an update on my progress on the murder case, of course," Logan replied with some surprise. "That is what you wanted, correct? And, like any good detective, here I am!"

"All right then, what's the update?" spat out Chief McGraw.

"Well, I did some research at the local library in newspapers dating back about 30 years or so looking for articles on missing persons. I ran across an article on a missing person—a priest at the Catholic Church here in Glendale by the name of Father Sebastian Antonio was reported missing. The article stated that Father Antonio had been scheduled to attend a retreat at the Our Lady of the Saints Monastery in Mount Scranton, but according to the story, he had never arrived," explained Logan.

"You think this guy is the body we found under the bell tower?" asked the chief with some interest despite himself.

"You remember the tarnished cross that was found next to the body?" reminded Logan.

"Sure, I do," retorted Chief McGraw, "but that's not a lot to go on."

"I've got more," answered Logan and leaned forward intently. "I drove to Mount Scranton and visited with the head priest, Father Andrew, to see if he knew anything more about the missing priest."

"And?" asked the chief impatiently. "Do I have to guess?"

"Chief, I'm surprised at you! You know what's mine is yours!" Logan said with a huge grin.

The chief just glared at him and waited.

"I got a copy of the retreat application that had been filled out by Father Sebastian. It gave the name of the seminary he had attended as a student, the St. Paul's Seminary of Serenity," Logan replied. "I thought it would be a way to find out more information on his background and family."

"And did you find out more?" was all the chief said, trying to hide his increasing interest.

"That's my next move, Chief," said Logan. "I'm heading there today."

Just then, their conversation was interrupted by a knock on the door. "Chief, I'm sorry to interrupt, but there's a hysterical old lady in the front office who says she just found a body in the park. Maybe you want to talk to her?" asked Sergeant Walker with a look that spoke volumes about how hysterical old ladies and painful corns should never meet.

Chapter 8

Chief McGraw stood beside Logan Stanton and watched with a look of disbelief as the body was transferred to the gurney. Who could have done such a terrible thing? He had seen some gruesome murders over the years, but none compared with this. Whoever the murderer was had mutilated what was once a face into nothing but an unrecognizable mass of flesh, bone, and blood. Obviously, it was a woman based on what was left of the rest of the body. But who did that belong to?

"What do think he used to do the job?" McGraw asked as he turned to Logan.

Logan simply shook his head and said, "Looks like some kind of blunt instrument—you know the standard description when the cops really don't have a clue."

McGraw snorted and glared at him. "I suppose you have some idea?" he bellowed.

"Keep your voice down, Chief, can't you see that little old lady over there is about to faint dead away?" responded Logan who managed a smile even under these circumstances.

McGraw looked over at the old lady and couldn't but think that he just wasn't paid enough to deal with old ladies, mutilated bodies, and smart-ass detectives. Retirement seemed like it was just a fanciful dream he once had.

He walked over to Mrs. O'Neil and spoke as soothingly as he could, which wasn't all that soothing. "Ma'am, how did you come upon the body?" he asked, trying to look like he really cared.

Mrs. O'Neil stopped shaking and crying long enough to blurt out, "I was taking my evening constitutional that I always take at this time of night, just before it gets dark because I don't feel safe walking after dark, especially in the park. No offense, Chief McGraw, but just how safe is our city? Not very much if this is any indication!" She had to stop as her voice started quivering again.

"Now, now, Mrs. O'Neil," McGraw answered, "we know this has been a shock for you. Rest assured that we will do all we can to catch the person who committed this horrible crime."

"See to it that you do!" said Mrs. O'Neil, pointing her finger at him while trying to smooth her disarrayed, freshly tinted silver-blue hair. She would have to make an extra beauty shop appointment just because this buffoon couldn't do his job!

While Chief McGraw was attempting to placate Agatha O'Neil, Logan Stanton took the opportunity to examine what was left of the dead woman. The first thing he noticed was no wedding ring. His eyes traveled from the lifeless hands up the arms. The woman had been wearing a floral dress of obvious cheap quality, which had apparently been torn during the struggle with her murderer. A tear on the left sleeve revealed some scars. He bent lower, lifting the torn material. Then, he whistled under his breath and called to Chief McGraw, "Sorry to interrupt you, Chief, when you are taking care of crucial police business, but I think you should see this!"

***

Dr. Morgan stared down at the body laid out on his examining table and shook his head. *Now, that is a dead body,* he thought. No doubt about what killed her— definitely a blunt instrument of some kind—used repeatedly when only one blow would have done the job. Whoever did this had hated this woman so much that one blow was just not enough. Or, maybe it was some random act of brutality committed by an insane person. Or better still, maybe an insane person who hated the woman. His mind kept trying to discover ways to explain the atrocity his eyes were unlucky enough to be taking in.

Chief McGraw strode into Dr. Morgan's lab with a mission. "Doc, any news on who she is?" was all he asked, trying not to look at the remains.

"Feeling a bit squeamish, Chief?" asked Dr. Morgan as he looked up at his visitor.

"Of course not, I'm just in a hurry to figure this whole thing out," retorted Chief McGraw rather defensively.

"Nothing yet, but I have sent her fingerprints to the state lab for analysis; they have access to the database that should tell us something about who she is," Dr. Morgan answered with a small smirk he was desperately trying to conceal.

"It will probably be tomorrow before I hear something," added Dr. Morgan.

"What about the needle marks on her left arm?" Chief McGraw interjected earnestly. "You didn't forget about them, did you?" he continued in the same breath.

"McGraw, do I tell you how to do your job?" Dr. Morgan squeezed out between his clenched teeth.

"I am just asking; you don't have to be so touchy!" Chief McGraw growled back as he stomped out of the room, slamming the door behind him.

***

Addison Temple was running late—she hated running late. Even worse, she hated over-sleeping. It always made her feel out-of-sorts, which was precisely how she was feeling as she swept into the office. Stella looked up from her computer and saw the signs. When Addison was in 'one of those moods,' she knew coffee—and as soon as possible—was the only way to go!

Stella quickly walked to the coffeepot, poured some into a mug, and followed her boss into her private office. "Running late again?" she asked with what she hoped was a nonchalant expression.

"How did you guess?" asked Addison while throwing her coat over a chair and sinking into her chair behind the desk.

"Oh, just a wild guess!" said Stella as she handed Addison the mug of coffee.

"Thanks, Stella!" said Addison and managed to smile. "What would I do without you?"

"Probably have to get your own coffee!" laughed Stella.

The sound of the outer office door opening and then slamming shut interrupted their laughter. Stella hurried out to see who was seeking their services so early in the day. She was somewhat taken back to see the police chief waiting rather impatiently at her desk.

"Good morning, Chief McGraw, what can I do for you?" asked Stella, noticing his agitation.

"Is your boss in? I need to see her right away," was all Chief McGraw said.

"I'll see if she is available," answered Stella as she reached for the phone.

"Never mind, I'll ask her myself," snapped Chief McGraw as he brushed past her desk and strode purposefully into Addison's private office.

Addison looked up from the file she was paging through as Chief McGraw burst into her office. "Chief, this is a surprise," as she closed the file rather quickly. "What brings you to our humble office? Don't tell me, you need our services?" she couldn't help adding with one of her most charming smiles.

"I'm here on official police business, Miss Temple, and I insist on nothing less than complete cooperation!" said Chief McGraw as he threw himself into the chair directly opposite her. His face spoke volumes about female detectives and how valuable they were to police business.

"Chief, don't you know by now that we are here to help in any way we can? Your problem is our problem. Cooperation is our middle name!" assured Addison in her best professional tone. She wondered what was up with the old coot. *We're probably getting too much dirt on one of his buddies who is involved in a case we are currently working on and he wants him left alone.* It wasn't unusual for the chief to pull some 'strings' when he felt the situation warranted it.

Chief McGraw opened his mouth to continue his "Need to cooperate with the police" speech; however, he paused just long enough to give Addison a sharp look. *Was she sincere, or just placating him?* Instead of the speech, he cleared his throat, reconsidered, and cut to the chase.

"Ms. Temple, my department is conducting a murder investigation and we have cause to believe that you may have information that can help us," stated Chief McGraw with some conviction.

"Why would you think that I would know anything about one of your murders?" asked Addison with annoyance in her voice.

"For the precise reason that the dead body is most likely one of your clients!" said Chief McGraw with obvious satisfaction.

Chapter 9

Addison could not keep a look of astonishment from her face. Which of her clients was the victim? How did it happen? When and why? All these questions began swirling in her mind. Somewhere, though, in the midst of her swirling thoughts, she couldn't help but wonder if she already knew.

The chief noticed that he had rattled Addison's show of confidence. *Finally, I got her!* He had been waiting to put one past her for a very long time. *Women—they were good for some things, but certainly not detecting!*

"Don't you want to know who it is?" asked McGraw with a smirk.

"Of course, if you are absolutely sure it is, or was, I should say—one of my clients, that is," Addison retorted.

"According to phone company records, you received some calls recently from a woman named Grace Evans, did you not?" questioned McGraw with a not-so-slight tone.

Addison felt a sinking sensation. So, it was true, her sense of foreboding had not been her imagination. The murder victim was Grace Evans. Out loud, she asked, "Why do want to know?"

"Because the body of one Grace Evans was found murdered in Ames Park last night. We have reason to believe you were working on a case with the dead woman," Chief McGraw explained in his most official jargon. "Did you know Grace Evans?" he went on to ask.

Addison felt the truth was the best alternative and admitted that yes, she knew Grace Evans.

"Ms. Temple, I am conducting an official police investigation and I want any information you have regarding the deceased as well as any case information you have involving her," the chief shouted as he leaned forward in his chair and shook his finger in her face.

"Chief McGraw, you know that I can't divulge that information due to client confidentiality," Addison forced a smile and refused to be intimidated by the blowhard.

"So, you admit she was a client of yours?" snapped McGraw.

"I admit no such thing," Addison snapped back.

"Well, trying to pull the 'client confidentiality card' won't work because your client is dead, therefore, confidentiality doesn't matter anymore," retorted the chief.

"Oh, but it does, Chief," responded Addison with another smile. "For you see, Grace Evans was not my client; however, she may be involved in a case I'm working on for a client and client confidentiality most certainly applies!"

Chief McGraw arose from his chair, nearly tipping it over backward in his haste. "If I find that you are withholding evidence regarding Grace Evans, I will see to it your license 'to detect' is revoked, little lady!" he sneered as he leaned across Addison's desk, his face inches away from her own.

Addison didn't move. She didn't need to. Her amber eyes did it for her. First, they flashed, then narrowed. "Chief McGraw, if you don't leave this office immediately, I will pick up the phone you are nearly sitting on and I will call my good friend, Judge Talbot, and request a restraining order for harassment be issued against you," she said with conviction.

"Restraining order! Are you crazy? I am the chief of police! No one places a restraining order on me, least of all a woman detective!" McGraw roared as he turned and stomped to the door.

"Shall we find out? Would you prefer to dial Judge Talbot's number, or shall I?" were Addison's parting words as the door slammed behind his formidable backside.

***

"Stella, I need you right away!" called Addison after she heard the slamming of the outer office door.

However, she needn't have called out as Stella was already poking her head inside to see if Addison was all right. "You all right, Boss?" she asked with a look somewhere between worry and amusement.

"Yes, I'm fine, but we need to do some digging and fast!" Addison answered as she reached for her coat.

"Get a hold of Farley as soon as you can and have him go down to the Medical Examiner's office and learn as much as he can about the murder of Grace Evans. It happened sometime last night in Ames Park. Have him report back to me on my cell phone as soon as he has anything." Addison was already almost out of the door.

"But, where will you be if I need you?" yelled Stella as the door was about to close behind her boss.

"Trying to find the dead woman's ex-husband!" was all Stella heard before the door snapped shut.

***

Thomas Evans threw the empty whiskey bottle across the kitchen, missing the garbage can, but conveniently not breaking as it landed on the rug beside it. The kitchen, and for that matter, the entire house was literally strewn with empty liquor bottles, beer cans, assorted empty pizza boxes, unrecognizable leftovers on dirty dishes, and dirty clothes added here and there, just to provide an additional artistic effect.

He was just about to try to get up and find another bottle of whiskey that he remembered hiding somewhere behind the cabinet that he kept his canned goods in—of which, there were very few—when suddenly, there was a knock at his front door. *Who was bothering him again? Wasn't it enough that he had that cop here this morning? Why doesn't everyone just leave him alone?*

He managed to walk to the door, but not until he swerved unceremoniously a couple of times. He flung it opened and blinked, then he blinked again. In front of him stood a gorgeous woman—probably the most gorgeous woman he had ever been lucky enough to meet, least of all on his own front doorstep. He cleared his throat and all he could say was, "What do you want?"

Addison stared at him. First, she stared at his face, took in his unshaven chin and his bloodshot eyes; after that, her eyes traveled downward and didn't stop until she reached his feet, which, by the way, were bare and rather dirty. Her mother had told her there would be days like this. Why couldn't she have done something more 'normal' for a living like teaching or even gone on to law school as her mother had wanted? She wouldn't be standing here now looking at a man who obviously had been drinking and who most likely did so frequently.

"I'm looking for Thomas Evans," said Addison with her usual air of confidence. "Are you Mr. Evans?" she went on to ask quickly.

"Who wants to know?" Thomas Evans replied, trying not to slur.

Addison handed him her card. Thomas Evans tried to focus on it while at the same time, trying to stay upright. "You're a female dick?" he slurred.

"You haven't answered my question," Addison ignored his comment. "Are you Thomas Evans?" she asked again.

Thomas Evans swayed as he answered, "What if I am?"

"Mr. Evans, I need to ask you a few questions," responded Addison with her best 'no-nonsense' voice.

"May I come in?" as she pushed past him into the house. She took one look and wondered why she had bothered. It would have been better to stand outside. The stench of liquor and filth nearly gagged her although she gave no visible sign.

Thomas Evans swung around to follow her inside and nearly fell but caught himself on the edge of the kitchen table. "Don't mind me if I have a little drink, do you 'female dick'?" he asked as he leered at her. His eyes traveled up her legs and stopped at her breasts. It certainly had been a while since he had seen a body like that.

"Mr. Evans, you have heard that your former wife, Grace Evans, was murdered yesterday?" Addison asked without a sign of noticing.

It occurred to Thomas Evans that perhaps this was not just a pretty face. "Yah, a cop stopped in this morning asking questions about her. I told him I hadn't seen Grace since we were divorced over ten years ago and didn't know a thing about what she had been doing with herself," as he reached for a glass and poured a sizeable amount of whiskey into it.

"Can you tell me anything about her at all?" asked Addison as she stood watching him take a long drink from the glass. She had better ask her questions quickly before the whiskey had its effects.

"What sort of things?" Evans asked as he slammed the glass down on the table. She was beginning to annoy him, and he didn't like being annoyed. "You're pretty nosy, aren't you?" he went on.

"Do you know anything about Grace's early life before she married you, for example?" Addison asked.

"What's there to know?" he sneered. "She knew her way around if you know what I mean," he added as a lustful look came into his eyes.

"Are you aware that Grace had a child that she had given up for adoption?" Addison said, thinking it might be better to get to the point as soon as possible.

Thomas Evans looked startled; that is, as startled as a drunk man can look. "Don't know anything about any kid or adoption," he said. "I think it's time you got out of here," he said as he tried to stand. "I don't want to get involved in any murder investigation."

"Mr. Evans, can you tell me about Grace's childhood or where she grew up?" Addison pressed on without moving. "Did she have any friends that she used to talk about?"

"As I said, it's time to go," answered Evans who managed to get up this time. "Are you leaving, or do I have to get tough?" he started, swaying toward her.

"Did Grace leave anything behind when you two broke up?" Addison said with no sign of fear.

"You think you're tough, don't you, 'female dick'?" yelled Evans who was standing directly in front of her now.

"Well, Mr. Evans, I have a job to do and I generally get that job done," she said, smelling his breath on her face.

Thomas Evans stared at her with his bloodshot eyes for a full minute trying to decide what to do. It was no good; he just couldn't think when he was drunk. Finally, he said, "OK, 'female dick,' you win." He turned around slowly and lurched toward a shelf in the bookcase that stood in the corner. He yanked out a photo album and started flipping through its pages until he got to one. He pulled out a picture and tossed it at her. It fell to the floor in front of her. Addison slowly bent and picked it up. It was a snapshot of a girl and two boys, all about 10 or 12 years old.

"That's the only picture I have of Grace when she was a kid. She never talked about her past. I think she said she had grown up somewhere upstate in the middle of nowhere," said Evans as he moved toward the table, aiming for the whiskey bottle.

"Where exactly upstate?" asked Addison looking at the three kids in the photograph. "And who are the two boys in the photo?" she asked.

"Haven't got a clue, nor do I really care," said Thomas Evans as he reached his destination of the whiskey.

"You haven't got a clue about where she grew up, or about the boys in the picture?" insisted Addison.

"The only thing I can remember is that the town had a girl's name, something like 'Shelby' or 'Shelly' or something crazy like that," replied Evans, filling his glass again.

"May I borrow this photograph for a while, Mr. Evans?" asked Addison as she began moving toward the door.

"Go ahead—I don't need it, or want it, for that matter," said Thomas Evans as he drained the glass once again, "as far I am concerned, she got what she deserved!"

***

Chief McGraw was mad, there was no mistaking it. When Chief McGraw got mad, he made sure everyone around him knew it. *That woman was going to be the death of him yet! What business did she have questioning anyone in connection with an official police investigation? Who did she think she was? She might be good-looking, but that's where it ends.*

He slammed out of his office on a mission. Desk Sergeant Walters looked up from his computer and wondered to himself which was worse, dealing with the chief in one of his 'moods' or dealing with a machine that had a mind of its own. Either way, it looked like a 'no-win' for him.

***

"Stella, has Farley called in today?" asked Addison as she breezed past her secretary's desk. "I really need to talk to him today if possible," she added.

"Farley just called and he's on his way to the office," answered Stella, seeing the excitement in her boss's face. "He should be here any minute," she went on to say.

"Good, I will fill you both in when he gets here," Addison called over her shoulder as she walked by to her private office. "Let me know as soon as he gets here; by the way, is there any coffee made?" she said as she threw her coat over a chair.

When her door opened a few minutes later, Addison was deeply engrossed in the photo she was studying and didn't look up. "Just put the coffee on the desk, Stella, and thanks," she said as she moved the magnifying glass even closer over the photograph.

"I don't do coffee, Ms. Temple," shouted Chief McGraw.

Addison looked up and noted the blood vessel near the bursting point on the chief's forehead. *Here we go again! He must have heard of my visit to Thomas Evans.*

"Why, hello Chief, it is so good to see you again and so soon," she almost purred and smiled at him. "To what do I owe this honor?" she continued, waving him into a chair.

"It appears my previous request to stop meddling in police business fell on deaf ears, Miss Temple," Chief McGraw ignored the chair and began pacing instead.

"I will have your license if you continue involving yourself in our police investigation!" shouted the chief as he shook his finger at her.

"I would never dream of doing such a thing, Chief, you know that," responded Addison while carefully placing the photograph under a stack of papers on her desk.

"You would certainly do so, and already have!" retorted Chief McGraw as his right eye started twitching.

"Chief, I assure you that I always follow any directive you may issue, and I'm surprised that you would even doubt my sincerity in this matter!" was Addison's only response.

A couple of minutes later—if anyone had been watching, that is—Chief McGraw was seen stomping out of the Temple Detective Agency.

***

Addison ran up the steps of the Glendale Public Library for there was no time to lose. She needed to know more about the names of towns located upstate with female names and needed to know in a hurry. She had already warned Farley that he must be available for some leg work on the Evans case.

She headed for the library's help desk and asked the attendant where the plat books were located. The librarian pointed her in the direction of the computer terminals as that information was now all computerized.

Addison settled in front of a computer and started searching for names of towns in the northern part of the state. *Thank goodness for computers*, she thought, as she worked diligently for the next hour or so.

She reached for her cell phone, but seeing the librarian's frown, walked over to the far corner and dialed Farley Brooks. Farley answered immediately. "What did you find, Boss?" he asked.

Addison filled Farley in on the quest for towns with female names and the connection to the Evans case. Farley agreed to leave immediately for Shelly and from there, would travel on to Shelby. "See what you can find out about Grace Evans and let me know as soon as you have anything," requested Addison. "I'll take Serenity myself," she added.

"I'm on it!" was Farley's reply.

Addison hung up her cell phone with a smile. Farley was such a good detective. He was always ready to take on any assignment she gave him. What a guy!

She was still marveling at her good fortune of having Farley in her employ as she came around the bookcase on her way to the front library entrance when she ran head-on into a man walking in her direction. Suddenly, she felt strong arms around her. She looked up into his face and her heart skipped a beat, or so it seemed—for holding her was none other than Logan Stanton, the one man who could shatter her cool professionalism as no other man could. She caught her breath. He smiled, his eyes twinkling, and asked, "In a rush, Miss Temple?"

"You may let me go anytime, Mr. Stanton, if you please," Addison managed to remind him breathlessly as it appeared Logan had no intention of letting her go anytime soon.

"Of course, Miss Temple, whatever you say!" he replied and abruptly let go, causing Addison to nearly stumble against the bookcase.

"What are you doing in the public library, Miss Temple?" Logan asked with one of his most charming smiles.

"None of your business and I might ask the same thing of you, Mr. Stanton?" said Addison as she tried to preserve what was left of her dignity.

"Now, is that anything to say to one of your fellow detectives?" teased Logan as he watched her reaction to their encounter.

"I really must be going, please let me pass!" replied Addison and felt herself blush. *What was wrong with her anyway? Why does this man always have an effect on her?*

"I'll let you pass on one condition and one condition only. That is if you promise to have dinner with me this evening," stated Logan with another one of his most disarming smiles.

"Mr. Stanton, you are totally impossible!" retorted Addison. "If you don't let me go this instant, I'm calling security!"

"I hate to disappoint you, Miss Temple, but this is a library and there is no security unless you call that middle-aged librarian a security guard?" asked Logan with a chuckle.

"Anything to get out of here! Pick me up at eight," said Addison through clenched teeth. She felt Logan's hands release her and she turned and ran out of the front doors, hearing his laughter follow her out into the brilliant sunshine.

Chapter 10

Logan watched Addison race out of the library and couldn't but admire the fine form she made. *What a woman, she even smelled like a woman,* thinking back to their brief encounter at the bookcase. He was definitely looking forward to their dinner date that evening.

Logan Stanton was by no means a 'saint' and had known his fair share of women in his time. He had, as they say, "Left his mark!" But, although he had enjoyed the company of many women, he was not one to become emotionally involved. No woman had truly touched that side of him—that is, not until now! There was something about auburn hair and emerald-green eyes that when paired with an undeniably attractive chassis with brains to boot, disturbed him.

Logan turned and made his way to the librarian's desk. "Could you tell me where the plat books are?" he asked the middle-aged woman who actually looked like a librarian in every sense of the word.

She pointed at the computers and said, "We use computers nowadays for plat information. There must be a great interest in plat books recently," she added.

"What do mean?" asked Logan with some curiosity.

"Well, you are the second person to ask about them this morning," the librarian replied.

"Has someone else been interested in plat books?" asked Logan and flashed his trademark smile.

"Of course; it's none of my business, but the young lady you bumped into over by the bookcase was asking about them just before you came in," said the librarian and managed an engaging smile of her very own.

***

Addison stood in front of her closet. What was she going to wear? She felt nervous, which was something she had never felt getting ready for a date before. *Damn him! Why had she said yes?* Of course, deep within her, she knew why. She wanted to say yes! She couldn't stop remembering how he had held her close and the way it had made her feel. It was as if his touch, even so brief, had ignited something inside her. She had never felt that way before.

Addison had dated several men, but none that could compare in masculinity or looks. *Let's face it, who could*, she asked herself. Logan Stanton was all man, there was no mistake. Quickly, she brought her focus back to her closet. She glanced at the clock on her bedside table and saw that it was already 7 o'clock. She had better decide soon as she guessed that Logan Stanton was not a man who liked to be kept waiting.

An hour later, Addison Temple opened her apartment door and her first official date with Logan Stanton began.

From the look on Logan's face at the sight of Addison, it was indeed a very satisfactory beginning!

Addison had selected a very feminine dress in shimmery green that matched her eyes and set off her auburn hair to perfection. Her hair shone in the light of the hall. She had taken great care with her makeup and as a result, looked even more beautiful, if that were possible.

If she had known how ravishing she looked at that moment, Addison might have felt some trepidation going out with such a man as Logan Stanton.

Logan felt something stir deep inside of him. He didn't know what it meant, or what it was, but he knew he had never felt it before. He smiled and said, "You look beautiful."

The only thing Addison could of think of saying was, "Thank you, so do you."

He laughed, then she laughed. "You know what I mean!" Addison said, feeling flustered for he was very handsome in his impeccably tailored dark suit, which showed off his broad shoulders and narrow waist.

"I brought you flowers," Logan said as he handed her a bouquet of red roses.

"How lovely, thank you so much! Let me put them in some water before we go. Won't you come in?" said Addison in a rather nervous voice.

Logan walked in and looked around. He noticed the neatness first, then the good taste in the décor. It was simply decorated, yet with definite style. He liked it. He walked over to the photos on the mantelpiece and picked up one of a man in his fifties. He looked familiar to him. Just then, Addison returned with the vase of roses.

"Is this your father?" asked Logan, turning around.

Addison placed the flowers on the coffee table and walked over to where Logan was standing. "Yes, that was my father, but he passed away a few years ago," she replied with a look of sadness in her eyes.

"I'm sorry, I didn't know," said Logan. "How did it happen?"

"He was working on a case—he owned his own detective agency—and was shot," said Addison quietly.

"You must miss him very much," said Logan gently.

Addison nodded her head and placed the photograph back on the shelf.

"Are you ready? We should probably be going. I made a reservation for 8:15 at Pascal's and you know how they feel about being late," said Logan, trying to lift her mood.

Addison nodded her head and he placed her wrap over her shoulders with care and escorted her to the door.

***

The food was excellent and so was the wine. Pascal's was Glendale's very expensive French restaurant—in fact, it was its only French restaurant—known for its food, service, and, naturally, its prices. Logan made sure the meal was to Addison's liking, leaving nothing amiss. He was an adept conversationalist and soon made Addison feel at ease.

She forgot how irritating he could be and before she knew it, she found herself laughing at his private eye anecdotes and thoroughly enjoying herself. The orchestra started playing when they were having their coffee. Logan held out his hand and asked, "Dance with me, Addison?"

Addison hesitated. Did she really want to be in those arms again? She didn't want to know the answer. So, instead, she smiled and nodded. They walked onto the dance floor. Soon, she was once again in his arms, this time moving in perfect rhythm to a lovely waltz. "I didn't know you could dance," she said for something to fill the silence that seemed to have descended upon them.

"There's quite a bit you don't know about me, Addison," was all Logan said. She could smell his aftershave lotion. It was tangy and yet had a hint of musk. They said little as they danced. When the dance ended, she felt somehow disappointed.

As they made their way back to their table, Logan and Addison passed by the table occupied by Jackson Smythe, Glendale's Assistant District Attorney, and his companion, an attractive young woman in her mid-twenties. Jackson Smythe was comparable to a 'blonde' version of Logan Stanton—however, without the personality. In fact, some might say Jackson Smythe had no personality—just a facsimile of one! He was undeniably good-looking and knew it. He had on several occasions taken Addison on dinner dates in the past at the suggestion of Addison's mother. One of the advantages he had going for him was being an acquaintance of Olivia Temple. Olivia and Jackson's mother were at college together and had remained friends, both having married and settled in Glendale. Olivia considered Jackson Smythe an ideal candidate for a son-in-law, an opinion she shared with her daughter on a regular basis. Addison, however, preferred to keep her relationship with Jackson on a 'friendship' basis, which was not the aspiration of either Jackson or her mother!

Jackson greeted them and asked, "Hello you two, out on the town tonight?"

Addison looked startled, but recovered quickly and replied, "Hello Jackson, it's good to see you. Have you met one of my colleagues, Logan Stanton?"

Jackson said with a smile that somehow didn't quite reach his eyes, "Yes, of course, how are you, Logan? It's been a while since I've seen you."

Logan smiled broadly and shook hands and replied, "Yes, it certainly has been a while," while thinking, *not long enough!*

Jackson turned to the young woman seated beside him and said, "I'd like you to meet, Chelsea Matthews."

Addison smiled and said, "Hello, Chelsea, it's a pleasure to meet you."

Chelsea nodded and replied, "Good evening, so good to meet you."

Logan merely smiled and said, "I already know Miss Matthews. How are you, Chelsea? You are looking lovely as usual." Logan was not wrong in his observation of Chelsea's appearance. She was lovely. Her dark hair and eyes were alluring, and, paired with her flawless complexion and obvious physical attributes, had undoubtedly attracted many admirers—among them, Logan Stanton.

Chelsea gave Logan one of her special "I remember our time together" smiles and answered, "I am doing well, thank you, Logan. It's been far too long."

Addison looked at Logan who quickly said, "We really must be getting back to our table. It was so nice to see you both."

Jackson exclaimed, "You mustn't leave just yet, join us for coffee before you go!" He motioned for the waiter and asked for two more chairs and ordered coffee.

Logan was about to refuse, but Addison interrupted and said smoothly, "Why, how nice, thank you, Jackson; we'd love to join you!"

If only looks could speak. The look Logan gave Addison would have spoken volumes!

***

On the drive home, Addison sat deep in thought. Logan also seemed to be in deep concentration. What had happened, she thought, they were both having such a wonderful time. It was as if they had been on a joy ride and now it was time for the ride to be over.

Logan helped Addison out of his car and walked with her to her apartment. "Would you like to come in for a nightcap?" Addison asked rather quietly.

Logan looked at her, then slowly his eyes traveled down to her mouth. Addison suddenly felt a bit breathless. What was he thinking, and why was he looking at her like that? Finally, Logan said, "I don't think I should, do you?"

With that, he thanked her, turned, and was gone.

***

Addison was running, trying to see who was turning the street corner ahead of her, but she could not catch up with the man. It was dark, and the light was bad. The dense fog made it difficult to keep her bearings. She kept running and running. Her breath came in gasps. Suddenly, out of the fog, a figure walked toward her. She stopped and waited. Finally, she would be able to see his face. There was a ringing in her ears that wouldn't stop; it went on and on. The figure stopped and turned away. The ringing became louder and louder. "Will you stop that ringing?" she shouted. Then her eyes flew open. She had only been dreaming and the ringing was her doorbell being rung incessantly by someone determined to gain entrance to her apartment. Who could be calling at this hour? Then, she looked at the clock and literally jumped out of bed. "Oh, my goodness, it can't be almost noon!" she said out loud. Addison yanked open the door and there stood the one person she really didn't need to see just then.

"Hello, mother, what are you doing here so early?" she said, then realized it wasn't early anymore.

"When I stopped at your office this morning and Stella told me you hadn't come in yet, I was worried. Mothers do that sort of thing, you know," replied Olivia Temple with a look of exasperation. "Particularly since your trusty secretary let slip that you had a date last night with Logan Stanton, Glendale's resident 'man-about-town!'" she added with relish. Olivia breezed into the apartment, taking a quick note that no men's clothing was visible.

"Mother, I am alone. There is no man lurking in my bedroom. You are welcome to check under the bed if you like," said Addison, trying to infuse some humor into her voice but failing rather dismally.

"Aren't you going to invite me to have breakfast with you since I'm here?" Olivia ignored her daughter's obvious lack of enthusiasm for her unexpected visit.

"Mother, I really don't have time for breakfast since, as you pointed out, I am late for the office already," Addison pointed out with as much diplomacy as she could muster in her present state.

"Oh, OK—if you must get ready, you must!" her mother deposited herself firmly on the sofa and waited.

"What is it, mother?" asked Addison knowing full well what it was, unfortunately.

"Well, how was your date with Logan Stanton? Or, do I have to beg?" asked Olivia in her best 'motherly' voice.

"There is nothing to tell, Mother; we had dinner and he brought me home, that's all," replied Addison as she went into the kitchen to put the coffee on. She was glad to avoid her mother's scrutinizing eyes. If there was one thing she knew about her mother, she could sniff out a story no matter what!

"You mean to tell me that was all there was to it? He didn't try anything, did he? You do know his reputation, don't you? Whatever possessed you to accept a date with him, anyway?" asked Olivia, finally pausing for breath.

"To answer your questions in the order received, 'yes,' 'no,' 'yes,' and, 'I don't know,'" answered Addison as she went into the bathroom and turned on the shower. Her mother's visit had disturbed her. Although her mother interfered, she did mean well. What she had said about Logan's reputation bothered Addison. She had to admit that her mother was right this time, Logan had a reputation with the ladies. Obviously, that included one Chelsea Matthews, if her female instincts were correct. And, her female instincts had never been known to fail her in the past. Was she also going to become just another statistic among all those other women that made up that reputation?

It was only until she heard her mother leave that she allowed herself to throw the bath soap against the far corner of the shower. *If that man thinks that I, Addison Temple, am going to become just another notch on his proverbial 'belt,' he had another thing coming!* Addison retrieved the soap and proceeded to scrub every inch of herself. By the time she finished, she practically shone!

Chapter 11

Logan Stanton drove his plain-Jane, unmarked, black 4-door sedan down the highway trying not to speed—at least not enough to get caught. He was in a hurry. As he drove along past rolling hills and fields of crops, his mind was occupied by where he was going. The St. Paul's Seminary of Serenity was located three hours to the north and the scenery along the way was gorgeous, if only he was paying attention.

All he could think of was the case. He woke up, ate, and slept the case. He felt like the dead priest was someone he actually knew personally. Why did this case mean so much? It was a case pretty much like a lot of cases involving a murder. Maybe it was so intriguing because the murder had taken place over 30 years ago. He only knew that the whole thing obsessed all his waking moments and he was determined to solve it!

Of course, he had to admit that the case was not the only thing that obsessed all his waking moments, particularly after last night's date with Addison. Why hadn't he kissed her, he kept asking himself? God knows, he wanted to! First dates with lovely ladies always meant first kisses in the past.

He must be losing his touch, or else? Or else what, he kept wondering?

Running into Jackson Smythe and Chelsea Matthews certainly had put somewhat of a 'damper' on the evening, he had to admit. Jackson was certainly 'full of himself,' that was obvious. It was also fairly evident that he admired Addison and would like nothing better than to become better acquainted. Judging by the way he had talked during their coffee; he already had become acquainted with her to some extent. This tidbit of information troubled him.

Of course, his prior acquaintance with Chelsea Matthews, although having meant nothing more than a brief 'fling' on his part, had not helped matters either. And, Chelsea's reaction to seeing him again might have been misconstrued, to say the least! He didn't give a 'hang' about what Jackson Smythe thought, but that was not the case where Addison was concerned. He had wanted to explain but somehow couldn't find the right words—at least, not yet.

The miles sped by until, finally, he turned his car into the gates of St. Paul's Seminary and drove down its tree-lined drive. The place was beautiful with a sense of serenity. What a great name for the town—Serenity. The town was set in the middle of nowhere and was surrounded by farmland for miles around. It must be one of those places where everyone knows everyone else along with their business, he mused as he parked his car in front of the main entrance. Students were walking between the many buildings, obviously between classes. Wow, the place must have looked like this 50 years ago—nothing had probably changed.

He made his way to the office and asked to see the senior priest. He was led into an inner office, which although sparingly furnished, exuded a sense of dignity and respectfulness. The priest seated at the large oak desk stood up and extended his hand. "Welcome to St. Paul's Seminary, I am Father Tobias. I believe you wished to see me?" said Father Tobias and motioned Logan to a chair. "What can I do for you?" he added as he returned to his seat.

"Thank you for taking the time to meet with me, Father Tobias. My name is Logan Stanton. I'm a private detective from Glendale working on a cold case from nearly 30 years ago that may involve a former student at your seminary," Logan explained. He went on to provide Father Tobias with the relevant details of the case.

"It is a possibility that the body found under the bell tower is that of Father Sebastian Antonio, who I believe attended this seminary as a young man. Do you remember him or have any records of his attendance here?" asked Logan with a hopeful look.

"I don't remember him; however, we will be happy to search through our files for whatever can be found on Father Sebastian," replied Father Tobias as he reached for the phone.

Soon, a priest knocked and entered the office. "Father Mason, will you search our files for any information we may have on a former student, Father Sebastian Antonio, who would have attended approximately 30 years ago? Please report back as soon as you can as this gentleman will be waiting," requested Father Tobias.

The priest nodded and retreated through the door as quietly as he had entered.

It seemed more like hours rather than minutes when finally, there was another knock at Father Tobias's door and the priest returned. He had with him a rather old manila file, which he handed to Father Tobias. "I am sorry; however, this file is all that could be found on Father Sebastian Antonio," said Father Mason with an apologetic smile.

"Thank you, Father, we appreciate your help," responded Father Tobias. "You may go."

Father Mason nodded and was gone.

Father Tobias opened the file and began paging through the few sheets that it contained. Finally, he looked up and said, "Mr. Stanton, I'm afraid there really isn't much here. Father Sebastian was a student here all those years ago. Unfortunately, the file includes only records of his grades and not much more. You may look for yourself," said the Father, handing Logan the file.

Logan paged through the file hoping for something that would shed some light on the priest and his background, but he had to agree with Father Tobias, there just wasn't anything. The priest saw his disappointment. "Mr. Stanton, perhaps all is not lost," he said with a smile.

Logan looked up and asked quickly, "What do you mean, Father?"

"Well, during that time, there was a priest here by the name of Father Joseph who oversaw the recreational and social activities of all of the seminary students. If anyone would have known any details about the students, he would have," explained Father Tobias.

"Where can I find this Father Joseph?" asked Logan excitedly.

"Father Joseph has long since retired and now resides at our local nursing home, Our Blessed Saints. His memory is not what it used to be, but perhaps he can be of some assistance," responded Father Tobias.

"Thank you so very much for your help," said Logan as he shook the Father's hand. "You may have just helped me take one more step toward solving a 30-year-old murder!"

***

Addison drove down the main street of Serenity and marveled at how the town seemed to have avoided the changes of time. The shops were colorful and quaint. People stood talking on corners. Cars were parked diagonally along the sidewalks and in double parallel in the center of the street. The town was not what she had expected when she had left Glendale early this morning. What would she learn here about Grace Evans? The town did not seem to match the woman Grace Evans had become.

She stopped in front of the Hotel Regency, a rather impressive name for what was actually the only hotel in Serenity. She parked and went inside. The man at the desk looked up from the newspaper he was reading and was pleasantly surprised by what he saw, for coming toward him was definitely a very attractive woman, which was not a common occurrence in Serenity. "May I help you, miss?" he asked and gave her his very best smile.

"Yes, you may," Addison answered, taking note of the man's reaction to her. "Do you have a room available for a few days?" she asked as she handed him her business credit card.

"We sure do. Do you want a king or queen-sized bed?" he continued as he took her card noticing the "Temple Detective Agency" on the card.

"Surprise me," replied Addison as she signed for the room. "Can you tell me where the public library is?" she went on.

"It's two blocks down and then a block north," said the clerk as he handed her the room key card. "May I take your bag up to your room for you?" he asked hopefully.

"No, thanks, I can take it," answered Addison, but softened her refusal with a smile.

He watched her walk to the elevators and wondered why a woman who looked like that would ever want to be a detective.

***

Logan Stanton drove directly to the Our Blessed Saints nursing home after leaving Father Tobias. He wanted to waste no time in seeing old Father Joseph. Father Tobias had given the impression that the old priest gets rather tired by the end of the day and, consequently, becomes a bit confused. Logan wanted to talk with Father Joseph before that happened.

When he arrived at the home, he was directed to a large common area where Father Joseph was sitting watching television. Logan sat down in a chair opposite him and introduced himself. Father Joseph turned his attention from the television and asked with some confusion, "Do I know you, my son?"

"No, Father, you don't know me. Father Tobias of St. Paul's Seminary suggested that I visit you because you may be able to help me with an investigation I am conducting," Logan answered.

The old priest stared at him for a time and then asked, "I don't know you, do I?"

Logan smiled pleasantly and said, "No, you don't. May I ask you a couple of questions about a seminary student you may have known about 30 years ago?"

Father Joseph nodded his head and replied, "You may, but sometimes, I don't remember very well, I'm afraid."

Logan leaned forward and asked, unable to keep the excitement out of his voice, "Do you remember knowing a student by the name of Father Sebastian Antonio?"

Father Joseph stared at him and said nothing for a long while. Logan watched and waited. He didn't want to rush the old priest for fear of confusing him even more.

Finally, Father Joseph said very softly, "Yes, I remember Father Sebastian—he was a good student who worked hard at his studies."

Logan couldn't believe his good fortune! Finally, a lead in the case. He bent nearer and asked, "Is there anything else you remember about him, Father? For instance, did he have many friends?"

The old priest nodded his head and said, "He had one friend in particular."

Logan asked quickly, "Do you remember the friend's name?"

Father Joseph shook his head, "No, I don't, it was so long ago. I'm sorry, but I'm getting rather tired."

Although Logan was disappointed, he thought it best not to press the old man for more at that moment. Instead, he said, "Thank you, Father; may I come back tomorrow and visit some more?"

Father Joseph murmured, "Yes, my son, do that."

Logan stood to leave. As he was shaking the Father's hand, the priest murmured something he could not quite make out. He leaned forward and asked, "What did you say, Father Joseph?"

Father Joseph repeated in a louder voice, "He always bothered me just a little, you know."

Logan paused—what was the old man saying? "What do you mean, sir?" he asked in surprise. "What bothered you about who?"

"Why, the young man we spoke about, of course, who else?" replied Father Joseph in a faraway voice.

"What was it that bothered you about him?" repeated Logan, trying to be patient but feeling more impatient every moment.

But Father Joseph was getting tired. "I don't remember, but there was something. I just don't know what it was. I need to sleep right now. I'll tell you later," as he drifted off in his chair.

Logan watched the old man sleep and wondered exactly what it was he meant. Hopefully, he would find out tomorrow.

***

Addison unpacked quickly and after a quick touch-up to her makeup in the bathroom mirror, took the stairs down to the hotel lobby. She nodded and smiled at the desk clerk as she walked past him on her way to the front entrance. Soon, she was driving down the street on her way to the library.

She walked in and headed straight for the front desk. The librarian in charge was very helpful and soon, she was searching the public birth records. She had decided to limit her search to approximately 50–55 years ago. It was amazing how many births took place during that period. She worked for an hour without success. She was about to give up until tomorrow when she saw what she was looking for—Grace Dorothea Evans. Grace was born in Serenity. The birth record gave a local address for her parents. Addison wrote it down quickly and stopped at the librarian's desk once more. Addison smiled and asked, "Can you tell me where 450 McKinley Avenue is?"

The librarian knew that area of town well and was able to provide detailed directions. Addison was on her way once more. Whenever she was 'hot on the trail' of a clue, she felt exhilarated. It was amazing how working on a case could take care of any 'emotional' aftermath that the date with Logan may have caused. What had she expected, anyway? He was an enigma and worse than that, he was an arrogant enigma who she just didn't need to deal with and, besides, she didn't have the time!

***

Addison drove up to 450 McKinley Avenue and parked in front. The house was small and definitely had seen 'better days!' The paint was faded and peeling. The grass needed mowing badly.

Addison got out of her car and walked up the sidewalk to the front steps. The place looked vacant. Addison felt deflated and quite sure that what she had thought was a lead would turn into a dead end. She rang the doorbell and waited. No sound came from within. She tried again and waited some more. Finally, she turned and started down the steps. She was about to walk around the side of the house when, suddenly, she heard someone say, "May I help you, miss?"

She looked up and saw an elderly woman waving at her from over the top of the hedge that divided the house from the one next door. Addison smiled, walked over to the woman, and then introduced herself. "My name is Addison Temple of the Temple Detective Agency in Glendale. I'm working on a case that involves the child that lived in the house next door about 50 or so years ago. Did you live next door all those years ago?" she asked, trying not to sound too anxious.

"Why, yes, I have lived in this same house for all that time. I do remember there was a family who lived there with a little girl. I think her name was Grace," the elderly woman answered.

Addison showed her the photograph she had obtained from Thomas Evans. "Is this the little girl, Grace?" she asked.

The woman put on her glasses and examined the photo closely. "Yes, that's Grace all right," she replied, looking up at Addison.

"Do you happen to recognize the two boys that are in the photograph as well?" asked Addison, trying not to sound too desperate.

"I don't remember their names, but I do remember that the three of them were always together, it seemed. They were great friends, always laughing and hanging around together whenever I happened to see them. The boys lived somewhere in town, but I never did know exactly where," said the old woman, handing Addison the photo.

"Thank you so much, ma'am, you've been very helpful!" replied Addison as she shook the woman's hand over the hedge.

Addison had hoped for more but was satisfied that at least she had traced Grace back to her childhood. It was a step in the right direction!

***

Logan Stanton drove to the Hotel Regency and parked. He was a mixture of emotions—excited because he might have a lead on Father Sebastian, but disappointed about having to wait to find if it was true or not. He needed a drink and some dinner. It had been a long day.

He checked in at the front desk and took the elevator up to his room. The room was clean and tasteful. Not bad for a town in the middle of nowhere, he thought as he washed and changed. He grabbed his room key, opened his door, and stepped out into the corridor just in time to watch Addison Temple walk down it toward the elevators. It was definitely her—there was no mistaking that body or that walk. He would have known both anywhere. He caught up with her and stood slightly behind her at the elevators.

She felt a presence behind her and turned around sharply only to be brought face-to-face with the one person she had decided to put out of her mind permanently.

They both looked at each other and said nothing. Logan looked into her eyes and felt something stir within him. He decided to break the silence first and said, "Hello there, what brings you to Serenity?"

Addison said nothing for a few seconds, then finally answered, "I'm working on a case. I might ask you the same thing, Mr. Stanton."

"So, it's 'mister' again? Why the change? I thought we were getting along rather well last night, didn't you?" Logan asked.

"I really think it best that we keep our relationship a business relationship only, that's all," replied Addison, looking a bit flustered. Just then, the elevator doors opened, and it was time to get on.

The doors closed on them and they were alone. "Then you do think our relationship was in danger of becoming a 'persona' relationship instead, 'Miss' Temple?" asked Logan with one of his smiles.

"I am really not interested in the type of relationship we have, Mr. Stanton," retorted Addison as she stepped out of the elevator, leaving Logan behind.

"Oh, but Miss Temple, I am," murmured Logan to himself as he followed her to the dining room.

Chapter 12

Addison had already been seated at a table in the far corner of the dining room. As the hostess, an attractive woman of perhaps 40 years of age, approached Logan, he smiled and said he was joining someone. She smiled and thought, if it was a woman, she was extremely fortunate to be dining with this gentleman. She watched as he strode across the dining room and, sure enough, he was joining a woman. Her feminine curiosity got the better of her and she took note of the woman—certainly a well-matched couple indeed!

Logan reached Addison's table and sat down. Addison looked up from the menu she was reading and glared at him. "What are you doing at my table?" she asked with a raised voice.

"Now, now, is that any way to treat a friend?" replied Logan with another one of his smiles. "I just thought since we both must eat dinner and since we are staying at the same hotel, why not have it together?"

In a moment, Addison's quiet evening had changed into one of inner turmoil. If she were completely honest with herself, she would have to admit that she was thrilled to see Logan again. Of course, she would never let him know that.

His ego was over-inflated already! Instead, Addison said rather primly, "I guess you're right, we might as well eat together based on the circumstances."

"There you go, time to be sensible!" said Logan as he was handed a menu by a waiter. "What are you in the mood for?"

It wasn't long before Addison started relaxing and enjoying herself once again in Logan's company. He really was a charming man; she couldn't help but think to herself. She also made sure to remind herself of his other alleged qualities, which included womanizing at the top of the list. She was not going to become another one of his many conquests—of that she would make very sure!

Logan couldn't resist bringing their chance encounter with Jackson Smythe during their night out. He said carefully, "It was certainly a surprise to run into Jackson Smythe. He gave the impression that he knew you quite well."

Addison, just as carefully, replied, "I am not sure exactly what you mean by 'quite well.' He has taken me out to dinner a few times. His mother and mine attended college together and have remained close."

Logan watched her fidget with the food on her plate. He wanted to reach across and grab her hand to make her stop, but something stopped him. Instead, he remarked, "He seemed to be enjoying Chelsea's company."

"Oh, you noticed that? I did too. They make an attractive couple, don't you think?" asked Addison, looking up.

Logan's expression remained unchanged, much to Addison's disappointment. He merely nodded and replied, "Yes, I totally agree with you."

The subject was changed after that. Their conversation turned to the cases they had worked on. They lingered over their coffee, talking. They talked of the 'quirky' clients they had run across along with the close calls they had been fortunate to survive. They discussed their techniques for detective work and for dealing with difficult clients. Later, Addison really couldn't remember exactly what they had talked about; all she remembered was that they had laughed a lot and before they knew it, the dining room was closing for the evening. As Addison was about to ask for separate checks, Logan interrupted and said to the waiter, "One check, please."

"I can pay for my own dinner," pointed out Addison in a hurry. "I'll write it off as a business expense."

"It's just as easy for me to do the same—that is, if that's what I will be doing," answered Logan while he paid the waiter and made sure to include a generous tip.

Logan escorted Addison to the elevators and they stepped on. Suddenly, Addison felt very nervous. Hopefully, their rooms were at other ends of the fourth floor.

Logan pushed number four and the elevator started rising.

Addison glanced at him, but she couldn't read his expression as he watched the illuminated number above the door change. The elevator stopped at number four and he escorted her off. "What's your room number?" asked

Logan, watching Addison fumble in her purse for her key card.

"I'm in 405," she mumbled as she searched, finally retrieving it from the far recesses of her handbag.

"Well, this must be my lucky day—I'm in 407, right next door!" said Logan with a twinkle in his eye.

Addison pretended not to hear as they walked down the hall to their rooms. She was about to insert her card when he reached over and took it from her hand. "Allow me," said Logan and inserted it for her.

There was a click and Logan pushed it open. "Thank you," said Addison as she stepped into her room. As she did, she brushed against him. She felt a quiver go through her body.

"Addison," was all he said.

She looked up at him. His face was unreadable. She felt breathless. He reached for her and then she was in his arms and she was being kissed as she had never been kissed before.

***

Addison was on the road early the next morning. Her mind wandered as she drove south toward Glendale. She couldn't stop thinking about last night and the feel of Logan's kiss. Logan had finally pushed her from him and said, "It's time we say good night."

Addison suddenly felt confused and then, embarrassed. So, all he had wanted was a bit of fun? How could she have been so stupid? Well, he had his fun and now it was over—for good! She said nothing as Logan said good night and went into his room. Perhaps if only Addison would have made better use of her detecting skills, she would have detected the controlled emotion in Logan's voice as he had pushed her away and would have maybe avoided the several anxious hours still ahead of her.

She drove straight through and made it back to Glendale in record time. She was glad to be back home and her routine. There would be no time to think and that is just what she wanted.

Addison walked into her agency and forced a smile. "Hi, Stella, how are things?" she asked, stopping at her secretary's desk.

Stella looked up, noticed the strain on her boss's face, but said nothing. "Everything's fine; Farley's back from those two towns you had sent him to. He found nothing on Grace Evans," she said.

"Oh, my goodness, I forgot to call him last night! I don't know what got into me. I did find out some more about Grace Evans in Serenity and should have let Farley know," Addison said, looking a bit sheepish.

"I'm sure Farley will understand, Boss. He's in his office now. I'll bring you both some coffee," replied Stella with a knowing smile.

"Thanks, Stella, that would be great. I sure could use some!" said Addison as she headed for Farley's office.

As Stella watched her boss walk down the hall, she thought to herself, *I think it'll take more than coffee this time*, as she wondered what had happened in Serenity.

***

Logan knocked on Addison's door as soon as he had showered and dressed the following morning. "Hey beautiful, how about some breakfast?" he called through the door.

The door opened and there stood a maid who doubtless had not been called 'beautiful' in some time with a rather perplexed look on her face. "Can I help you sir?" she asked.

"Oh, hello there; where's the young lady who stayed in this room?" asked Logan with one of his customary smiles.

"She checked out early this morning, sir, that's why I'm cleaning the room," answered the maid who was obviously not immune to Logan's smile.

Logan was not smiling as he thanked her and returned to his room, slamming the door behind him.

Later that morning, Logan was still not smiling after he got in his car at the Blessed Saints Nursing Home parking lot. Father Joseph had experienced a setback overnight and was even more confused than he had been yesterday. Logan had no hope of finding out more information from him for at least the next few days.

***

It can be accurately stated that Logan made even better time than Addison driving back to Glendale. He paid no attention to speed limits because he simply had better things to think about and even more important things to do. *What made her think she could kiss me like she had last night and disappear without even a goodbye the next morning?* She must think he's just some guy she can use and toss aside. Well, she's going to get a piece of his mind. No woman had ever done that to him and no woman ever would, if he could help it! And, he thought he was actually falling for her—that vain, beautiful, know-it-all woman—the same one, he couldn't help thinking, who had those beautiful eyes, that gorgeous hair, lovely mouth, exciting personality, and, as he found out last night, possessed an undeniable passion and sensuality like no other woman he had known. And, then, there was that Jackson Smythe! Where did he come into the picture? What were Addison's feelings toward that fair-haired, egotistical buffoon?

Oh, damn it all, he adored her, and he knew it! It occurred to him about the same time it occurred to the cop who was parked on the side of the highway—which ran from Serenity to Glendale—that the speed limit was for everyone.

***

Farley Brooks smiled at Addison as she walked into his office. "Hi there, how did it go for you in Serenity?" he asked.

"Actually, it went quite well," answered Addison as she sat down across from his desk. She couldn't help noticing what a mess it was—there were scraps of paper, post-its stuck on top of post-its, and notebooks thrown in randomly for good measure all over the top of it. Farley certainly worked differently than she did, but his methods still produced, for which she was very grateful.

"I'm really sorry that I forgot to call you last night after I got back to my hotel," said Addison in an apologetic voice.

"It just slipped my mind. I hope you didn't waste too much time at the places you visited?"

"Don't worry about it, it didn't take all that much time and effort on my part," Farley assured her. "What did you find out?" he went on to ask.

Addison filled Farley in on what she had learned about Grace Evans and then showed him the photo of a young Grace with two boys. "I haven't been able to trace who the two boys are in the photograph yet, but I think it would be a great help to the case if I could," explained Addison.

Just then, Stella came in carrying two cups of coffee. She handed each of them a cup and announced to Addison, "That chief of police is here again, Boss." Stella did not conceal her general feeling of disapproval in his untimely interruption in their workday.

Addison thought, *now, what does he want?* She got up, taking her cup with her, and resignedly went into her office.

***

Addison walked into her office expecting a difficult conversation and she was right. Chief McGraw was pacing back and forth in front of her desk. When he spotted her, he stopped and didn't waste time getting to the point. "Miss Temple, I need your cooperation on the Grace Evans investigation and I don't want any trouble," he said in his best 'chief of police' voice.

Addison went over to her desk and sat down. "I thought we already discussed this, Chief McGraw," she said in a very tired voice. "How could I possibly help you in your investigation?"

Chief McGraw shook his finger at her and said with relish, "This time, Miss Temple, your client is involved in a police investigation and you must cooperate with the department."

"Chief, I explained all that to you already, Grace Evans was not my client," she retorted, feeling exasperated at his total stupidity. Why were cops so dense, she wondered to herself.

"I am not talking about the victim, Miss Temple, I am talking about your client, Ava Richardson," replied Chief McGraw with satisfaction.

"What are you talking about?" Addison asked incredulously.

"Then, let me explain, Miss Temple. Ava Richardson is wanted for questioning and has disappeared. We need all the information you have on the woman, so we can try to locate her as soon as possible. This time, you must cooperate, or suffer the consequences!" answered McGraw, punctuating his words with his finger once again.

Addison looked at Chief McGraw and wondered who it was that had hired this guy as the chief of police; however, thinking better of expressing her question out loud, she reached for her phone instead. "Stella, would you please bring in the file on Ava Richardson?" she said as she saw the look of triumph cross Chief McGraw's corpulent face.

***

Olivia Temple was nothing if not resourceful. She was much like her daughter in that respect. After she left Addison's apartment that day, she was determined to find out as much as she could about her daughter's date with Logan Stanton. But, how to go about it, she wondered?

She knew the Stanton Detective Agency was downtown because she had driven past it many times on her way to lunch with friends. She also knew it was located not far from a small bar/cafe that had been owned by the same proprietor for years, which was often frequented by the locals at lunchtime. It was not the type of place she usually would have been 'caught dead' in, but due to the dire circumstances involved, she decided to make an exception this time.

At around noon, Olivia Temple was seen entering Sammy's Bar and Grill wearing sunglasses and a rather large floppy hat. She quickly entered and sat down in a corner booth. A waitress walked over and asked in what Olivia considered 'standard' vernacular, "What can I get you?"

"I'll just have a cup of coffee," replied Olivia, trying to hide behind the menu.

The waitress took one look at her and thought, *we sure get all kinds in here*, as she walked away.

Olivia sat drinking her coffee watching everyone who came in. Sammy's Bar and Grill was indeed a busy lunchtime spot. She was on her third cup when she saw Logan Stanton walk in and head for the bar. As soon as he sat down on a stool, the bartender went over to him and greeted him with a smile. Logan ordered and started chatting with the waitress who also had seen him come in. Although she was most likely on the far side of 40 years, she laughed and talked as gayly as a 20-year-old girl. What was it about that man that women found so irresistible, Olivia couldn't help wondering?

Olivia grabbed her handbag and left the booth. She walked up the bar and stood next to Logan and said to the waitress, "May I have my check, please?"

The waitress looked a bit annoyed at having her conversation with Logan interrupted, but said instead, "Sure thing, ma'am," as she walked away to get it.

Olivia glanced at Logan and asked, "Why, aren't you Logan Stanton?" in her best 'surprised' voice.

Logan turned his head, smiled, and answered, "Why, yes, ma'am, I am, but I don't think I have had the pleasure."

"You don't know me, Mr. Stanton, but I've heard a great deal about you. You see, Addison Temple is my daughter and has talked of you quite often," Olivia said and held out her hand.

Logan smiled even wider, shook her hand, and said, "How good to meet you, Mrs. Temple! I didn't know that Addison had such a lovely mother."

Olivia gushed and said, "Please call me Olivia, Mr. Stanton."

"Only if you'll call me Logan," replied Logan, his eyes twinkling as they watched her.

"By the way, Logan, my daughter informed me that you two went out on a date the other night. Did you enjoy yourselves?" asked Olivia as innocently as she could, which was definitely a stretch for her.

Logan smiled and couldn't resist saying, "I can truly say that the date changed my life."

Olivia stared at him and her mouth opened and then shut. When it opened again, she asked, "Why, whatever do you mean?"

"Only that I enjoyed myself a great deal. Your daughter is not only beautiful on the outside, but she is also beautiful on the inside, which is something rare in the women of today's world—don't you agree, Olivia?" he asked as innocently as he could.

"Oh, yes, of course, I agree totally. You're right, of course," Olivia managed to say.

"In fact, I was delighted that we ran into each other again the next day in a town up north where we were both working on cases," Logan said, watching her reaction.

The reaction soon came. Olivia's surprise was instantaneous. "You saw each other in another town? It is certainly a small world, isn't it?" was all she could say.

"You are so right, Olivia. And to add to our delight, we found that we were even staying at the same hotel and in rooms next door to each other," Logan added with some amusement.

"Really? How nice," answered Olivia, turning a bit red. Just then, the waitress returned with her check. Olivia paid quickly and prepared to say goodbye.

"It was a pleasure to meet you, Logan," said Olivia as she moved toward the door.

"Olivia, the pleasure was all mine, I assure you!" replied Logan with one of his smiles. This time, it was a genuine one.

Chapter 13

Addison left her apartment and drove to her office in her Ford Mustang just like she did every morning. It was a beautiful day much like a lot of other beautiful days she had admired in the past. However, this particular day seemed just a little more beautiful than the other ones had been. She really didn't stop to analyze the reason or reasons that this might be the case. If she had done so, she may have been somewhat surprised, to say the least. But, she didn't; instead, she just let herself enjoy the moment, which was something she had never had much time to do in her life.

She simply adored driving her car. She had not taken the purchase of her very first sports car lightly. Unlike most women, Addison knew a great deal about cars. Her father had taught her a thing or two about engines, including horsepower, exhaust systems, and the like. He had always been a 'Ford' man and because she had wanted to hold true to his memory, had chosen a Ford product.

She had been very pleased with her choice. Heads turned when she drove her 'Venetian red' Mustang down the street. She loved that! Not because she was conceited, but because she thought it was liberating in some way. The drive to work ended too quickly and soon, she parked her 'baby' and walked into the building. Stella greeted her with her usual warm smile and said, "Good morning, Boss!" Stella continued in a softer voice, "I hate to break the news so soon, but your mother is waiting in our office. She seems very anxious to see you."

Addison's smile vanished. Her beautiful day had just become cloudy with a chance of rain. She loved her mother dearly, but she did have the uncanny ability to appear at the most inopportune moments. Some of her unannounced visits could even create a tangled state of affairs, which typically wound up upsetting both daughter and mother.

Oh well, there was nothing to do, but talk to her! Addison squared her shoulders, stuck out her pretty chin, gave Stella a knowing wink, and walked into her office. Stella smiled back and shook her head.

Olivia Temple was seated busily flipping through a magazine, which she had taken from a nearby table. When she saw Addison, she flung it down and got up immediately to give her daughter a hug. "How are you, darling?" she asked, looking closely at Addison's face trying to see if anything really was wrong.

"Hi, mother; I'm just fine, why do you ask?" ventured Addison with just a little reluctance. *Here we go*, she thought!

"You'll never guess who I ran into yesterday," said Olivia without even a pretense at subtlety.

Addison sat down at her desk and decided to face the inevitable head-on and replied, "I have no idea, Mother, but I'm sure you're going to tell me."

"Logan Stanton, of all people!" stated Olivia, totally ignoring Addison's response.

Addison had been busily turning on her computer and had begun reading emails while half-listening to her mother. Her hands stopped, then her head turned toward her mother. "What did you just say, Mother?" she asked incredulously.

"Why, Logan Stanton, of course. You know, the man you had a date with the other night. Surely, you haven't forgotten about him? Especially since he tells me that you two stayed in the same hotel the next day and out-of-town, I might add!" said Olivia with the triumphant tone of an investigative mother in search of news of her daughter's love life!

Addison cleared her throat. She cleared it again. Finally, she asked, "How in the world did you manage to run into Logan Stanton, of all people?" She watched her mother fidget with her handbag and wondered what her mother was up to once again.

"Well, I was uptown on my way to do some shopping. I walked past that little bar and grill on the way—you know the one, I think it's called Sammy's Bar and Grill. I suddenly felt hungry and realized I hadn't had my lunch, so I went in. Lo and behold, there sat Mr. Stanton about to order his lunch," explained her mother with a slightly raised voice that Addison did not miss.

"In other words, Mother, you planned on stopping at Sammy's around lunchtime with the hope of finding Logan Stanton there. Admit it, Mother!" replied Addison sharply.

Olivia hesitated and looked a bit sheepish, which was difficult for her, and said, "Yes, if you must know! I was

111

only doing it because I wanted to protect you from him—you know his reputation as well as I do."

"I am fully aware of his reputation, Mother, and besides, there is nothing between Logan Stanton and me. We are just in the same business, that's all. We happened to run into each other while we were both working on cases. We had no idea we were booked in the same hotel. That's all there was to it!" explained Addison with a firm voice.

Olivia took a close look at her daughter. She recognized her daughter's stubborn look and thought it best to leave her well enough alone—for now, that is. "All right, if you say so, Addison, but I still say there is more to this 'relationship' than meets the eye!" She got up, gathered her things, and walked to the door.

Before she opened the door, she turned and said, "By the way, I have changed my mind about him. I think he is a perfectly charming man!" And out of the door went her mother, leaving a very relieved, not to mention very confused daughter in her wake!

***

Logan walked into the office and looked around. It was just as he expected—professional, neat, and classy. The woman at the front desk looked up as he walked in. Then, she looked again. She smiled and asked, "May I help you, sir?"

"Yes, you can, miss. It is 'miss,' I hope?" Logan smiled and asked.

Stella Downey automatically put her hand up to her hair, then realized what she was doing and stopped herself.

She couldn't help thinking, *I hope my lipstick looks fresh enough!* "Why, yes, it is Miss, since you ask," she answered with another smile.

Logan smiled again and asked, "Is Miss Temple in?"

Stella asked, "Miss Temple?"

Logan replied, "Yes, Miss Temple—you know, your boss."

Stella recovered her composure and replied, "Oh, that Miss Temple. I'll see if she's in. Who shall I say wishes to see her?"

"Please tell her that Logan Stanton wishes to see her," answered Logan with a slight smirk, knowing full well that she must have recognized him.

Stella nodded and picked up her phone and said as softly as she could, "Boss, Logan Stanton is here and wants to see you." She listened for a few seconds, then put down the receiver.

"Miss Temple will see you now, Mr. Stanton," said Stella, trying not to look too interested.

Logan smiled again and thanked her. "By the way, you look lovely today," he said as he walked to the inner office door.

Stella watched him walk across to Addison's office door. She pulled out the mirror in her desk drawer and looked at herself.

***

Addison had no time to collect herself before she found Logan Stanton standing in front of her desk. She stared at him, he stared at her. Neither spoke for a few moments. She didn't know what to say. He didn't want to let slip how good it was to see her again. He had always been attracted to her beauty, but since their last meeting a few days ago, he knew there was so much more to her than just her beauty. She had spirit and intelligence. What's more, she had independence and integrity. Qualities like these were difficult to find in anyone. She was what he liked to call a 'complete package' kind of woman. He was the first to speak, "Hello, Addison, it's good to see you again."

Addison swallowed and managed to say, "You, too. This is certainly a surprise. To what do I owe the honor of this visit?" She began to busily rearrange the papers that were strewn across her desk.

"May I sit down?" asked Logan, indicating a chair across from her.

Addison blushed and replied, "I'm sorry—yes, of course, have a seat."

Logan sat down, noticing Addison's obvious nervousness, which was certainly not at all like the Addison he was beginning to know. He decided to open the conversation. "I'm here actually on what might be called personal business."

Addison stared at him and asked, "Personal business; what kind of personal business could we have?"

Logan replied, "Why, Addison, you wound me! How can you even say that after our last meeting? By the way, I knocked on your door the next morning to ask you to breakfast, but the maid told me that you had already checked out. Why the rush?"

Addison said as matter-of-factly as she could, "I had to get back to the office as soon as possible. I had a case that needed my attention."

Logan looked amused and said, "I was very disappointed. I had my heart set on sharing my eggs and bacon with you!"

Addison thought it best to divert Logan's attention to the reason for his visit. "What is the personal business that you wish to discuss?" she asked, using her professional voice.

Logan's face was the picture of innocence as he answered, "I'm not sure how to say this, but your mother decided she had to talk to me and cornered me at Sammy's Bar and Grill. She decided to 'grill' me instead, and I quite innocently let slip that we had stayed at the same hotel while out of town. She seemed to me a bit upset by that fact. When she pried the additional room locations out of me, she displayed even greater angst!"

Addison watched him and did not buy the 'innocent' act for a minute. If there was one thing that Logan was not, it was innocent. She was quite sure anything he did or did not do was planned with great care. He most likely led her mother on with his usual suave charm. Why else would she have changed her opinion of him so completely? She decided the least said about her mother's involvement, the better!

Addison replied with as much casual interest as she could muster, "Yes, I believe Mother did mention in passing something about seeing you the other day. I am sure she has totally forgotten about it by now. She's so occupied by her volunteer work as well as her friends."

Logan smiled broadly, "Well, if you say so—you know her best, of course. I just thought it best if you hear about it from me first, but I see I was not quick enough!"

"Is there anything else? Because if there isn't, I really need to get back to work," said Addison, trying to appear as normal as she could while realizing that normal was not even remotely possible when it came to her interactions with Logan Stanton.

Logan stood up and leaned over the desk and looked into Addison's eyes. He looked as if he was about to say something, but instead straightened back up. His eyes caught a glimpse of a photograph that was lying on top of a file folder. He picked it up and studied it carefully. Finally, he asked, "Where did you get this photograph?" in a serious voice.

Addison collected her senses and answered, "That is confidential case information, please give it back."

"But, don't you see, Addison—I think I recognize one of the people in the photograph as being someone on one of my cases!" Logan said with great excitement.

Chapter 14

Addison stared at Logan and asked, "Are you sure? Which one of them do you recognize? I bet it's the girl because she is the victim in a murder case that's under investigation. Her picture as an adult has been in the newspaper." She couldn't keep the same excitement out of her voice.

"No—actually, it's one of the boys," replied Logan, as he pointed to the boy on the right of the girl.

"One of the boys?" asked Addison with an incredulous voice. "I don't believe it!"

They both bent over the photograph. Logan said again, "Yep, that's a younger version, but I'm sure the adult photo I have matches perfectly!"

"Who is he? Does he live here in Glendale?" asked Addison hurriedly.

"Well, actually, he used to a long time ago," answered Logan. "I believe he was a priest at Our Lady of the Lake Catholic Church here in Glendale about 30 years ago."

"A priest? Do you mean to tell me that he is the priest who was murdered all those years ago and whose remains were found under the church bell tower a couple of weeks ago?" Addison asked with total amazement. Her green eyes were sparkling by this time.

"Yes, that is exactly what I think! However, you haven't told me who the other two people are. Fill me in, woman!" laughed Logan, grabbing her hand and holding it.

Addison looked down at their hands but did not pull away. At that moment, she felt so connected with him that she didn't want anything to spoil it. Instead, she said, "The girl is a young version of the woman by the name of Grace Evans who was found murdered in the park a few days ago!"

Logan whistled and said, "No kidding! How did you find this photo? You had better start from the beginning!" He sat down and pulled her into the chair beside him, still holding her hand.

Addison proceeded to fill Logan in about Grace Evans and the case she was working on for Grace's daughter, Ava Richardson. Logan listened intently; his eyes glued to Addison's face. Although he was listening closely, he couldn't help noticing how excitement seemed to enhance her features.

After Addison finished talking, it was Logan's turn to talk about the case he was working on involving the dead priest. He explained how Chief McGraw had asked that he give a hand with the investigation. Addison couldn't help but notice that McGraw was willing to have a male private investigator help. McGraw just moved up her list of male chauvinists!

They both agreed that there must be a connection between the two cases. Logan said, "Addison, it only makes sense that we should work together on these cases from now on."

Addison looked down at their hands, which were still together. She looked into his eyes and nodded.

***

Addison drove to the trailer park located on the edge of town. The trailer park had a questionable reputation, primarily due to the drug busts that had taken place there over the past few months. She parked in front of a mobile home at the end of the second row and took a good look at the home. It definitely had seen better days. The metal on the sides of the trailer was a faded green and she could see holes in the skirting along the front.

Addison walked up to the front door and rang the doorbell. She could hear a television blaring inside. She rang again, this time holding the button in. Finally, there was the sound of steps and the door opened. In the doorway stood a large man with a rather untidy appearance. His hair, which came to his shoulders, looked unwashed. He started swaying as he stood there blinking in the sunshine. "What do you want?" he asked with an unmistakable slur.

"I'm looking for Sam Richardson. Are you Sam?" Addison asked, watching him sway.

"Who's asking?" asked the man, trying to focus on his visitor.

Addison was beginning not to like the way the man was looking at her. She decided it was better to get to the point as quickly as she could before the guy got any ideas. She handed the man her business card and waited. He held it up close, then he tried holding it at arm's length. Nothing appeared to work for him. Finally, he gave up and threw it on the ground.

"Just tell me who you are and what you want," he said in a surly voice.

"My name is Addison Temple. I own the Temple Detective Agency in town," answered Addison in a friendly voice, hoping to appear less threatening.

The man stared at her and finally said, "I'm Sam. What do you want me for?"

"May I come in? I'd rather speak to you inside," replied Addison.

"Suit yourself, lady!" said Sam Richardson as he turned and went inside.

Addison followed him into the trailer and shut the door behind her. The first thing she noticed was the smell. It reeked of liquor. She thought, *why is it I'm always questioning drunks? First, it was Thomas Evans, and now Sam Richardson.* Sam grabbed a beer off the table and swayed over to the couch. The television was still blaring.

Addison asked, "Would you please shut that thing off, so we can talk for a few minutes?"

Sam grunted and picked up the remote and turned the television off. "Make it snappy, I haven't got all day!"

Addison sat down at the kitchen table as gingerly as she could, trying to avoid looking at what was on top of it. She asked, "Can you tell me where Ava is?"

Sam snorted and started laughing. Addison asked, "What's so funny?"

"Well, lady, for one thing—I haven't seen my wife for a few days, and for another, I could care less!" sneered Sam, taking a healthy swig of his beer.

"I see. I would like to talk with her as soon as possible. Do you have any idea where she might be?" asked Addison with a determined voice.

"You must be that detective she told me she had hired to find her real mother," replied Sam.

"Yes, I am, but I can't discuss the particulars of the case with you without Ava's consent," said Addison carefully.

"Hell, I don't need to 'discuss' anything because there's nothing to discuss! If you think you know everything about your case, you are so wrong, lady!" said Sam with a laugh.

"What do you mean?" asked Addison, watching him take another hefty swig of beer.

"Ava pulled a fast one over on you, missy! She told you she needed to find her birth mother because she needed genetic information to save her little boy's life, didn't she?" he asked.

"I can't divulge that to you, Mr. Richardson," replied Addison, suddenly feeling a strange foreboding.

"You don't have to! I know she did because she bragged about her scheme to me. I hate to blow your case wide open, lady, but she doesn't have a son. We haven't got any kids! She lied to you about the reason for finding her old lady. And, that's just the half of it—there's a lot you don't know about your client," stated Sam with a laugh.

"Why would she lie to me, if she did?" asked Addison.

"That's something you're going to have to ask her. That is if you can find her. The only thing she was good for was the money she was going to come into and in a big way! She

121

had a plan, you know! All I care about is getting my share!" answered Sam as he picked up the remote again and turned the television back on again.

***

Logan's mind was swirling as he drove toward the Our Lady of the Lake Catholic Church. Could it really be true that his cold case from 30 years ago could actually be somehow connected to Addison's case? It was unbelievable! Addison appeared to be as astonished as he had been when he had identified one of the boys in the photograph. But, where do they go from here? Addison had opted to go see Ava Richardson's husband to see if he knew where she might be. He had suggested that he visit the current priest at the Catholic Church to learn what he could tell about the deceased Father Sebastian—if the body that was found under the bell tower was indeed Father Sebastian, that is. He felt sure that it was. He was going to find out, no matter what!

He reached the church, parked in the front, and went inside. The church had been built just prior to the bell tower project, which was about 30 years ago. The church board had left the bell tower project for last with the reasoning that should the church construction costs exceed their budget, the bell tower construction could be delayed until sufficient funds were available. However, fortunately—at least for the board, if not for Father Sebastian—the church construction came in under budget, allowing the completion of the bell tower as planned.

The church was truly beautiful inside. The stained glass on the windows along with several statutes of divine saints added to the atmosphere of serenity. The design was simple, yet appealing. He looked for the office and located it in a corner. He went inside and found a priest seated at the desk in deep thought, staring down at a book open in front of him.

Logan cleared his throat and the priest started visibly and looked up. He looked shocked at the intrusion. He was a man of about 50 years of age with graying dark hair of average build. Logan quickly walked to the priest and extended his hand. "Hello, you must be Father Douglas?" he asked with a quick smile.

The priest shook his hand and answered, "Yes, I am. May I help you?" he asked with a curious look.

"I'm Logan Stanton of the Stanton Detective Agency and I wonder if I could ask you a few questions if you have some time?" Logan asked.

"Of course, please have a seat," replied Father Douglas, indicating the chair across from him.

Logan sat down and said, "I'm here investigating the case of the body that was found beneath the bell tower a couple of weeks ago."

Father Douglas fingered the cross that hung around his neck. He said, "I really don't know any more than what I have already told the police, which is very little."

"I'm actually assisting the police department in the matter and there's been a recent discovery that may impact the case. I believe it may be possible to identify the body based on new evidence," explained Logan.

"New evidence? What sort of new evidence?" asked Father Douglas with a surprised look.

"It's a long story, but suffice it to say, a positive identification might be possible," answered Logan with a confident look.

The priest simply nodded and waited. "Can you tell me if you know the names of any prior priests who were assigned to this church?" Logan asked.

Father Douglas rose and walked to the window that looked out onto the location of the bell tower. He turned and looked at Logan, then said, "I really don't know their names, however, I'm sure the church board would have that information in their files."

The priest returned to his desk and sat down again. "I'm sorry, Mr. Stanton, but I am rather busy just now. Is there anything else you need to ask me before I must say goodbye?" asked Father Douglas with an expressionless face.

Logan looked at Father Douglas carefully, then said, "Yes, there is just one more question. Did you ever meet the priest who you replaced when you first came to the Our Lady of the Lake Catholic Church?"

Father Douglas looked at him for several seconds, then answered in a quiet voice, "Father Sebastian was already gone when I arrived here, therefore I never knew him."

***

Logan pressed the buzzer precisely at 9 o'clock the following morning and waited. Hearing no answer, he gave it another push. From somewhere inside, he heard movement, then the door opened. He couldn't help smiling;

who could if the person who opened the door looked like Addison Temple!

She looked beautiful, as usual. She was wearing a dark blue suit, which emphasized her narrow waist and gorgeous figure. Addison smiled and said, "Sorry, I hope I didn't keep you waiting."

She noticed how he was always dressed so impeccably. His suit was expensively cut of good quality material, which made him look even more attractive. Of course, she would never let him know that!

Logan smiled back and said, "It was worth the wait."

Addison felt herself blush and locked her apartment door behind her and they walked down the hall to the elevator.

Soon they were on the highway heading north to Serenity, this time together. Logan had explained about the old priest, Father Joseph, who was in the nursing home there and how he had taught Father Sebastian when he had been a student at the seminary. Logan had suggested they go visit him again to see if he was able to remember more about his former student. Addison brought the photograph along as well, just in case it would help.

The time went by quickly as Logan drove. Addison was beginning to feel a bit more at ease in Logan's company and started to enjoy herself. Although the trip took over two hours, it seemed like no time before they were turning into the gates of the Our Blessed Saints Nursing Home.

Father Joseph was sitting in the sun on the back patio when they asked an attendant where they might find him. Logan and Addison greeted the elderly priest. Logan introduced Addison and explained why they had come to see him. Father Joseph didn't appear to recall Logan's prior visit at all.

Addison and Logan looked at each other in frustration and disappointment. What should they do? Addison opened her handbag and took out the photograph of young Grace Evans and the two boys. She bent down next to Father Joseph's chair and asked gently, "Father, do you recognize any of these three young people?"

Father Joseph's attention had been diverted by a couple of blue jays at the bird feeder at the edge of the garden. At Addison's words, he turned his gaze to her. She held the photograph out.

The priest looked at the photo. Suddenly, his eyes lost their vacant look. Logan and Addison looked at each other, then back at Father Joseph. The priest was talking to himself in a low voice. They leaned closer to hear when suddenly Father Joseph yelled out, his voice shaking, "He was a disgrace to the cloth! He should have never been a priest!"

Logan and Addison did their best to calm the old priest, but he continued to shout, "He was a disgrace, he was a disgrace." A couple of nurses came running at the sound.

Father Joseph began struggling with the nurses, trying to get out of his chair. His face was red with his exertions. Just as suddenly as he had started yelling and struggling, he stopped. Father Joseph had died.

Chapter 15

Addison and Logan talked little on their trip back to Glendale. Their hopes of learning more information from Father Joseph were gone.

Logan looked at Addison sitting beside him. Her nearness stirred him. He reached over and took her hand. She turned her head to look at him and smiled. She was glad she was with him. Working together on the case had brought her a new understanding of him as a man and as a detective. The arrogance she once thought he had was now replaced by confidence. He was a smart man, there was no doubt of his capabilities as a detective. But she had discovered that he was also a very compassionate man who was capable of understanding and sensitivity.

Logan dropped Addison off at her office when they got back to Glendale a couple of hours later. He squeezed her hand and said, "I'll call you later."

Addison nodded and said, "Thanks for taking me with you today."

Logan smiled and replied, "Of course, I wouldn't have it any other way."

Addison watched him drive off heading down the street toward his office. She turned and walked up the steps into her office. Stella looked up as she entered, smiled, and asked, "How was the trip to Serenity?"

Addison shook her head and answered, "Not so good, I'm afraid." She then filled Stella in on what happened to Father Joseph at the nursing home.

"Unbelievable! Then you weren't able to get any information from the priest before he passed away?" Stella asked.

"Nope. He got so agitated at seeing the photograph that it was impossible to calm him down to talk to him," answered Addison, disappointment showing in her voice,

The sound of the phone ringing interrupted their conversation. As Stella answered, Addison walked into her private office.

She had just sat down when Stella buzzed. "Boss, Ava Richardson is on the phone," she said excitedly.

Addison quickly picked up her phone and said, "This is Addison Temple."

Ava Richardson spoke quickly in a strained voice, "Miss Temple, I really need to talk to you right away!"

"Ava, the police are looking for you. They want to question you about your mother's murder," said Addison just as quickly.

"Miss Temple, I didn't do it, I didn't kill my mother!" exclaimed Ava in a frightened voice.

Addison tried to calm her by saying, "The police only want to ask you some questions, that's all, Ava."

"They want to pin the murder on me, I know it! It starts with questions, but it will wind up with me being arrested, I just know it!" answered Ava, her voice starting to quiver.

"OK, take it easy, Ava. Come to my office as soon as you can, and we'll talk about it," said Addison in a reassuring voice.

But Ava wasn't having it. "No! I'm afraid the police will find me," she said, almost crying.

Addison thought quickly and asked, "All right, Ava, where do you want to meet?"

There was a pause on the other end of the phone, then Ava said, "How about outside at the Catholic Church? I can meet you on the south side in the garden."

Addison thought for a couple of seconds and asked, "OK, Ava, when do you want to meet?"

"How about later tonight after dark? I can be there at 10 o'clock," answered Ava in a rush.

"I'll be there, Ava," said Addison as she hung up.

***

Logan drove up to the Our Lady of the Lake Catholic Church and parked. He hoped he wasn't too late. According to the church calendar, the quarterly meeting of the church board was being held that afternoon at 5 o'clock and he wanted to be there.

He walked inside and headed for the meeting room. He heard voices as he approached and opened the door. The board members were assembled at the large round table in earnest conversation. They looked up as he entered. He sat down in a chair as quietly as he could and waited for an appropriate moment to intervene. They reached the point in the agenda for 'new business' and since what he wanted to discuss was 'new,' he thought it was probably the best time as any to introduce his reason for being there. His luck had held out and apparently, Father Douglas did not attend the quarterly meetings.

"Excuse me, gentlemen, may I address the board?" asked Logan, standing up and approaching the group.

One of the members who appeared to be chairman, smiled and asked, "Yes, of course, I assume you are here on a church matter of some kind?"

Logan nodded and explained, "Yes, I am. My name is Logan Stanton of the Stanton Detective Agency. The chief of police has asked me to help with the investigation currently underway involving the body that was recently discovered beneath the church bell tower. I wonder if I could ask some questions?"

The chairman, a gray-haired older man, looked at the other board members. They all nodded in agreement. He then indicated a vacant chair at the table. Logan smiled his thanks and sat down.

"I'm not sure how we can help you, Mr. Stanton, but we certainly will try," said the chairman.

"I want to question you about Father Douglas. Could you tell me something about him? What was his background, where did he grow up and go to school, what seminary did he attend, that sort of thing?" asked Logan hopefully.

The board members looked at each other and then back at Logan. "Why do you wish to know this information?" asked the chairman.

"It's just routine, sir. I'm investigating anyone that is associated with your church. Since Father Douglas is the current priest, I must learn more about him as well," replied Logan.

"Of course, I understand," said the chairman as he nodded his head. "Father Douglas was assigned to us about six years ago. I do remember that he did come from somewhere within the state."

"Was his background checked prior to his assignment?" asked Logan.

"All priest assignments are handled by our bishop who is responsible for conducting any background examinations," replied the chairman.

Logan looked disappointed at the news. "Would you check any files you may have on him and let me know if you have any additional information on him as soon as you can? It's very important to the investigation," he asked.

He agreed to do so but felt it may not prove to be very productive. Logan left his card and thanked the board for their time. He had reached the door when the chairman called out, "Mr. Stanton?"

Logan turned and asked with some surprise, "Yes, sir?"

"You do realize that this is Father Douglas's second assignment with us, don't you?" asked the chairman.

Logan's surprise was instantaneous. "Second assignment? What do you mean?" he asked quickly.

"I know the rest of our board may not realize this, but since I am probably the oldest member here, I have the distinction of knowing that Father Douglas was assigned to our church previously," answered the chairman.

"When was this?" asked Logan, trying not to show his excitement.

"It was immediately after the disappearance of Father Sebastian. I remember him distinctly. We needed a priest immediately and when we contacted our bishop, we were fortunate to get a replacement within a couple of weeks because Father Douglas was willing to come to us right away, which was a great help due to the circumstances," he explained.

Logan stared at him and probably for the first time in his life, had nothing to say.

***

Logan dropped by Addison's office hoping to catch her in. Stella was just about to leave for the day and was surprised to see him.

Logan greeted Stella warmly and asked, "Is your boss around, or has she gone home for the day?" as he glanced toward Addison's office.

"I'm sorry Mr. Stanton, but she's not here right now. She probably won't be back tonight. I do know that she has an appointment to meet with a client later this evening," answered Stella with a smile. He was so good-looking; she couldn't help herself.

Logan asked, "Can you tell me who the client is, Stella?"

Stella looked at him and shook her head and replied, "I'm sorry, but that's confidential. The boss would have 'my hide' if I did!"

"Stella, you do know that your boss and I are collaborating on a case together, don't you?" he asked, giving her one of his best smiles.

Stella hesitated, clearly confused about what to do. A few moments later, she said, "All right, Mr. Stanton, since she did share with me that you are working together on a case, I guess it's all right."

"Thanks, Stella, so who is the client? Don't keep me in suspense!" asked Logan a bit impatiently.

"She's meeting Ava Richardson around 10 o'clock tonight," said Stella.

"Ava Richardson! Are you sure?" asked Logan, worry showing on his face.

"Yes, I'm sure because Ava called here today and wanted to meet Addison. She wanted to meet somewhere private is all Addison told me; she didn't say where, though," answered Stella, getting worried herself at the sight of Logan's face.

"Stella, you have got to show me Ava Richardson's file right away," said Logan emphatically.

"Is there something wrong?" asked Stella.

"Only that Ava Richardson is the police department's prime suspect in the murder of Grace Evans!" replied Logan grimly.

Chapter 16

Stella handed over Ava Richardson's file without hesitation. Besides, Logan was not taking 'no' for an answer judging by the look on his face. Logan grabbed it and quickly flipped through it. "If you hear from Addison, try to reach me on my cell phone right away," said Logan and gave her his cell phone number.

Logan ran out of the office before Stella had a chance to open her mouth.

***

Logan parked his car in front of the trailer house and got out. He could hear a television blaring inside as he walked up to the front door. He knocked and waited. There was no sound of movement. He tried knocking again. There was still no sign of life. Finally, he tried the doorknob and it was unlocked. Logan walked inside cautiously.

Logan saw a man of about 35 years of age slumped over the kitchen table. He slowly walked over to him and asked, "Are you Sam Richardson?"

The man did not stir. Logan tried again and repeated, "Are you Sam Richardson?"

There was no response. Logan shook the man's right shoulder hard and said, "Wake up!"

The man mumbled something inaudible. Logan lost his temper and slapped him hard across the face. The man opened his eyes and tried to focus on who had hit him, but his eyes kept shutting. Logan slapped him again, this time even harder. The man's eyes snapped open, staring at Logan. Logan asked again, "Are you Sam Richardson?"

Sam managed to nod his head; at least, it looked like a nod. "Where's Ava?" asked Logan without wasting any time.

Again, there was no response. Logan yanked the man out of his chair, tipping it over in the process. "Either you tell me where she is, or I'll make sure you won't wake up for a long while!" threatened Logan.

Sam Richardson managed to open his eyes. Logan shook him, and he mumbled again. Sam started laughing. "What's so funny?" asked Logan, shaking him.

"She let me in on it, you know," slurred Sam.

"Let you in on what?" Logan answered as he slapped him hard.

Sam stopped laughing and managed to say, "Who are you?"

"Never mind, what were you let in on?" asked Logan, threatening to slap Sam again.

"Don't hit me again! It was Grace's idea at first, but Ava got drunk one night and bragged that she would get even more dough. That's where I came in; she said she'd cut me in if I kept my mouth shut," said Sam, beginning to sweat.

"Do you mean blackmail?" asked Logan, shaking Sam again.

"Yah, yah, that's what I'm talking about," yelled Sam when his head stopped shaking.

"Who was being blackmailed?" asked Logan.

"Ava wouldn't tell me anything else, I swear!" said Sam as Logan raised his hand to hit him again.

Disgusted, he threw Richardson on the floor and walked out, slamming the door behind him.

***

Addison had some time to kill before meeting Ava Richardson and decided to look at the site where the dead priest's remains had been found. She had not yet visited the site since Logan brought her in on the case.

She parked her car in front of the Our Lady of the Lake Catholic Church and walked over to the fenced-off area around the bell tower. The fence surrounded a gaping hole left by the bulldozer that sat nearby, which had been brought in for a clean-up following the incident with the drunk's car.

Addison tried to get a closer look and stepped as near to the edge as the fence allowed. Unfortunately, however, in her eagerness, her foot slipped. Suddenly, she felt a hand grab her arm and pull her backward.

She screamed and turned to look at who had just saved her from falling head-first into the hole. It was Father Douglas!

"Oh, my goodness, Father Douglas, I'm so glad you were there!" said Addison with relief.

"Are you all right?" asked Father Douglas, still holding her arm.

"Yes, Father, I'm fine, thanks to you!" replied Addison as she smoothed her dress and her hair.

"You are welcome, I am glad to be of service," said Father Douglas with a slight smile.

"My name is Addison Temple, I'm a private detective working on a case," explained Addison.

"Since you are here, I am assuming it is the case involving the body found under our bell tower?" asked Father Douglas.

Addison nodded and said, "Yes, I was visiting the scene to get a 'feel' for what might have taken place all those years ago."

"And did you get a 'feel' for what happened?" asked Father Douglas with a curious tome.

"Not really. Did you know the priest who you replaced when you came to the church?" asked Addison as she and Father Douglas walked back to the front entrance.

"I'm afraid I did not. I arrived just after he had disappeared. I believe his name was Father Sebastian," replied Father Douglas.

"Yes, that was his name. We're trying to find what we can on the priest's background. It's too bad you never met him," said Addison, watching him closely.

"I am sorry that I cannot be of more help, Miss Temple," was all Father Douglas said.

"Well, I must go. Thank you again for saving me from what would have been a nasty fall!" said Addison as she walked toward her car.

As she walked away, she remembered what the old priest, Father Joseph, had said before he died, "He should not have been a priest." *Had Father Joseph been referring to Father Sebastian, or could he have been talking about someone else?*

Father Douglas stood and watched her drive away. He didn't move until her car was out of sight.

Chapter 17

Addison drove away from the Catholic Church deep in thought. Her conversation with Father Douglas had disturbed her. There was something that bothered her about him, but she just couldn't put her finger on it. She shook her head, trying to clear her thoughts, and parked down the street. She reached for her cell phone and called Stella.

"Hi, Stella, it's me. Are there any messages?" asked Addison when Stella answered.

"Boss, Logan was here. He was very anxious to find you once he learned you have an appointment to meet Ava Richardson. He insisted that I show him Ava's file. I hope that was all right?" asked Stella with some hint of anxiety in her voice.

"Sure, Stella, don't worry about it. We're working on the case together," answered Addison.

"I'm not sure what it was all about, Addison, but Logan stormed out of here as soon as he read through the file," said Stella.

"Did he say where he was headed?" asked Addison, feeling a bit worried.

"No, he didn't say a word at all. He just ran out of the door!" answered Stella.

***

Logan had read Ava Richardson's file. Why had he rushed out? Where could he have gone? She started her car and continued down the street. There was one place he might have gone in such a hurry. She turned her car in the direction of the east edge of town.

Addison had hoped she had seen the last of Sam Richardson and his trailer, but here she was again. She drove up and parked. Same trash outside and she guessed there would the same trash inside, most likely even more.

She went up to the door and knocked. The television was blaring. She could see the lights were on inside, so she knocked again. Finally, she heard a muffled voice.

Addison turned the knob and pushed the door in. There was Sam Richardson slumped on the couch. He was trying to get up, but his legs appeared to have their own ideas. Addison walked over to the television and shut it off. Sam looked up at her and said as best he could, "Hey, pretty lady, what do you think you're doing shutting off my TV?"

"I'm trying to talk to you, that's what I'm trying to do, Mr. Richardson," answered Addison as she stood in front of him.

"So, what do you want? I thought I got rid of you once already," said Sam, still trying to stand up.

"Did a detective by the name of Logan Stanton come to see you today?" asked Addison as she picked up a kitchen chair that had been tipped over and sat down.

"I want another drink," said Sam as if he hadn't heard her.

140

"Mr. Richardson, I think you've had enough," replied Addison as she watched Sam try to maneuver himself out of the couch.

"I don't care what you think, lady," said Sam as he finally stood up, swaying, and made his way to the kitchen table. He grabbed a glass, poured some whiskey into it, and gulped it down.

"Yah, a guy was here earlier looking for my wife. I told him she wasn't here, and I didn't know where she was. I'm telling you the same thing, so you might as well get out of here," said Sam as he got up and weaved his way back to the couch.

Addison stood up and walked over to him. Sam had started to pass out. She spoke sharply to him, "Mr. Richardson, wake up."

Sam opened his eyes and managed to mumble, "You've got things all wrong, pretty lady!"

"What do mean, I've got things all wrong? Wrong about what?" demanded Addison, going nearer to him.

But Sam Richardson was sleeping like a baby.

***

By the time Addison left Sam Richardson's trailer, it was nearing 10 o'clock. She turned her car back toward downtown. It was turning dark by the time she parked in front of the church. She walked to the south side of the church and looked around. There was no sign of Ava Richardson. Addison walked over to the lantern light that illuminated the south walkway to look at her watch. It was a few minutes before 10 o'clock. Addison walked to the edge of the garden and stood there waiting, trying to see if anyone was approaching in the darkness.

As Addison contemplated where Ava Richardson was, Father Douglas was contemplating who Addison Temple was waiting for at this time of night in the south garden. He walked to the window and stood back out of the light shining into the window from the outside lantern.

In a couple of minutes, a woman appeared from around the corner of the church. She walked quickly toward Addison and as she passed beneath the light of the lantern, Father Douglas saw the woman's face. He recognized Ava Richardson.

***

Addison turned and saw someone approaching. As the person walked closer, she could see by the light coming from the lantern that it was Ava Richardson. Even in the faint light, Addison could see that Ava was distressed. She clasped and unclasped her hands.

Addison suggested that they sit on the bench not far away. They moved over to the bench and sat down. Ava kept glancing at the church, apparently watching for movement inside the church. "Are you expecting someone?" asked Addison, watching her closely.

"No, no one at all—I'm just being careful, that's all," was Ava's hasty reply.

"Well, what did you want to talk about?" asked Addison.

"I didn't kill my mother; you must believe me!" said Ava desperately.

"Why should I believe you?" asked Addison.

"Because I had no reason to kill her. Why would I kill the mother I just found?" Ava asked.

"Where were you at the time your mother was killed?" asked Addison, instead of answering Ava's question.

"I was at home with my husband," answered Ava.

"I talked with your husband and he said he hasn't seen you for quite a while. He also said you lied about why you wanted to find your mother. You don't have any children and, naturally, it follows that you have no children who need their medical history," replied Addison in an unbelieving voice.

"Sam is lying, he's a drunk and that's what drunks do!" answered Ava as she stood up and started pacing back and forth.

"If you didn't murder your mother, Ava, then who did?" asked Addison, watching Ava.

"There was someone who had a reason to want my mother dead," replied Ava as she stopped pacing suddenly.

"Who do you mean?" asked Addison, standing up and walking over to her.

"Father Douglas," answered Ava as she glanced back at the church windows.

"Why Father Douglas?" asked Addison.

"Yes, why indeed?" answered Father Douglas as he walked toward them out of the shadows.

Chapter 18

Logan returned to his office as quickly as he could. His secretary, Madeline Avery, was busy at her computer as he breezed by her desk. Startled, she looked up just in time to see him close his office door.

She got up and walked over to the door and went inside without bothering to knock. Madeline Avery was not someone who stood on ceremony for she had been Logan's secretary since he had opened his agency. Besides, she had known Logan and his family for years, way before Logan became the man he was today. Madeline was what one would describe as a 'mature' lady with graying hair that always had that 'fresh from the beauty parlor' look, which, in her case, was exactly what it was. Yet, one should not be deceived by her conservative appearance; she also knew how to handle Logan's most difficult clients and was not hesitant to do so.

Logan looked up as Madeline walked in. Madeline noted a new look on Logan's face—that of worry and concern. "What can I do?" asked Madeline, watching Logan rummaging through the various files and documents on his very messy desk.

"Avery, where's the information we received from the church board?" he asked, frowning and throwing papers around in a frenzy.

"I put it on your desk so that you would have it when you came in," Madeline replied calmly. She had seen her boss in states of anxiety before, but never like this. She walked over to the desk and started sorting through what was remaining on top of it and that had not yet made its way onto the floor.

Madeline picked up some sheets that had been clipped together and handed them to Logan who was still busy rooting around. "Here it is," she said.

Logan grabbed the papers from Madeline and sat down. "Care to tell me what this is all about?" asked Madeline.

Logan glanced up at her and answered, "Sorry, Avery, it's just that I'm in the middle of something."

"I understand, just let me know if I can do anything else," replied Madeline with a smile and a nod of understanding. She knew when to leave Logan to it.

***

Logan started reading through the information received from the Our Lady of the Lake Catholic Church board via email late that afternoon. It contained what they had managed to gather on Father Douglas. He paged backward through the recent stuff until he got to the older pages from around the time of Father Douglas's hire.

The credentials that Father Douglas had provided at the time of his hire about three decades ago consisted of the bare minimum of information. The seminary he had attended was listed as being closed. It had been located in a small town called St. Michael. Logan noticed the year of graduation. The signature on the diploma looked somehow familiar to him. Where had he seen that signature before?

He searched for the Father Sebastian case file. He quickly rifled through it until he got to the photocopy of the application for the retreat that Father Sebastian was to have attended 30 years ago. Attached to the application was a copy of Father Sebastian's theological degree from the St. Paul's Seminary of Serenity. Logan looked closely at the signature. Then he held it next to the copy of the degree awarded to Father Douglas. The two signatures were identical. He looked carefully at Father Douglas's degree certificate and noticed although the names of the seminaries were different, the wording used on each of the degree certificates was identical. The year was the same on both; however, the months and days were different.

Could Father Douglas be the other boy in the photograph? Had Father Douglas and Father Sebastian been childhood friends along with Grace Evans? If so, why had he lied to cover up that fact?

He grabbed his suit jacket and headed for the door. "Avery, I'm going to pay a visit on Sam Richardson who lives in a trailer on the edge of town. Call me on my cell phone if you hear from Addison Temple. It's urgent that I speak with her!" said Logan as he ran by her desk.

***

Logan broke all speed limits on his way to Sam Richardson's trailer. The only thing he cared about was talking with Sam Richardson. The chances were, though, that Sam was still so drunk that he wouldn't even be able to talk, but he was going to try anyway.

He reached Sam Richardson's trailer in record time. The lights were still on and everything looked lifeless just as it had before. The television was still blaring, and he heard it even before he had switched off his car.

Logan ran to the door and threw it open. Sam Richardson was sprawled across the kitchen table, sleeping. Logan yanked him out of the chair and slapped him hard across the face. Sam's eyes flew open and stared at him. "What are you doing here again?" asked Sam with fear in his eyes.

"I'm here because I want to know more about Ava's blackmail scheme," said Logan as he pulled Sam's face within inches of his own.

"I told you all I know!" answered Sam, looking more and more scared.

"Either you tell me all of what you know, and right now, or I'll beat it out of you!" said Logan, looking straight into his eyes.

Seconds went by. Finally, Sam nodded. Logan released him and Sam fell back into his chair. "I need a drink," said Sam.

"Not until you talk," answered Logan as he grabbed the bottle out of Sam's reach.

Sam cried, "But, I need a drink, I'm starting to shake!"

"Too bad, start talking or you'll shake even more," replied Logan, without feeling.

"OK, OK, what do you want to know?" said Sam, holding his hands, trying to keep them still.

"Who was Ava blackmailing? Don't tell me you don't know!" said Logan.

Sam looked at him and finally said, "A priest at the Catholic Church. She said she had him right where she wanted him."

"What did she have on him?" asked Logan.

Sam looked at the bottle next to Logan and licked his lips. Finally, he said, "Ava's mother told her that she had read about the body found under the church tower. She came back to Glendale because she figured she could make some easy money. That's all Ava told me; I swear!"

Logan stared at him, his mind processing what Sam had said. So that must be it! Grace Evans had been blackmailing Father Douglas because he had killed Father Sebastian. She had read about it in the newspapers and decided to cash in.

"Why would Grace tell Ava about the blackmailing scheme?" asked Logan, picking up the bottle.

Sam's eyes did not leave the bottle. "Grace told Ava that Father Douglas was her father. My guess is she didn't want Ava messing up her plan. She told Ava that she threatened the priest she would tell the church board that he had a daughter if he didn't pay up."

"But, why would Ava mess up the plan?" asked Logan, confused.

Sam laughed and answered, "Grace probably was afraid of Ava. You see, Ava must have threatened to kill her if she didn't get a cut."

Logan shook his head and asked, "Why would Ava want to kill her mother?"

"Not until you give me the bottle!" said Sam.

Logan hesitated a moment, then handed over the bottle.

Sam grabbed it and took a swallow then wiped his lips with the back of his hand. Then he said, "Because Ava's crazy like a loon! She was diagnosed with something called manic-depression years ago. I tried to get her help, that's when she walked out and has been on the run ever since!"

Logan stared at him, then ran out without another word.

Chapter 19

As Father Douglas moved out of the shadows, both Addison and Ava got to their feet when they saw the gun he held in his right hand. Father Douglas motioned with the gun for them to sit back down on the bench. They slowly sat back down again.

"What do you want?" asked Addison, watching him closely.

"What do I want? Why not ask Ava? She's the reason I'm here," answered Father Douglas with a look of malice in his eyes.

Addison looked at Ava with the unspoken question. Ava said nothing for a few seconds. Finally, she said softly, "Father Douglas is my father."

Addison stared at her. She couldn't believe what she had just heard. It just didn't make sense. How could she have missed this? Grace Evans had not divulged to her who Ava's father was. In fact, Grace had not wanted to pursue the subject at all.

Addison asked, "Ava, how do you know that Father Douglas is your father?"

"Because my mother told me that he is," answered Ava.

Suddenly, Father Douglas gave a loud laugh. It startled them, and they turned to look at him.

"What's so funny?" asked Ava, clearly becoming upset.

"Because, crazy woman, I am not your father!" answered Father Douglas with a look of amusement.

"You must be! My mother told me she grew up with you. You got her pregnant and then entered the priesthood to avoid responsibility," said Ava as her voice rose sharply.

"Are you sure that's what really happened?" asked Father Douglas with a slight smile.

"But it must have happened that way. Why else would you agree to pay me money to keep quiet about it?" asked Ava disbelievingly.

"Pay you money?" interjected Addison with a confused look.

"Yes, Miss Temple, your client is blackmailing me, didn't you know?" said Father Douglas.

"What does he mean, Ava?" asked Addison, looking at her curiously.

Ava reluctantly admitted, "Yes, I am. My mother was behind it all, she just brought me in on it."

"You mean to tell me Grace was blackmailing Father Douglas after all these years because he was your father? Stop and think about it. Why would she have waited nearly 30 years to blackmail him now?" asked Addison incredulously.

Ava looked at Addison with confusion, then turned her gaze on Father Douglas. "I hadn't thought of that," she said, still trying to understand. Her whole body had started to shake.

Addison looked at Father Douglas. "Why did you let Ava blackmail you for something that wasn't true?" she asked.

***

Father Douglas smiled and said, "Because Ava's reason was invalid."

"But, why would Grace lie to Ava about the reason?" asked Addison, feeling very confused.

"Because she thought she could get away with giving Ava a smaller cut of the money, of course!" explained Father Douglas.

"A smaller cut?" asked Addison, shaking her head.

"Yes, being accused of fatherhood would need to be proven. Grace knew that I wasn't the father, so she lied to Ava because even if Ava got it into her head to accuse me of being her father, it would require a paternity test and since she knew that I wasn't Ava's father, she also knew that I would fail the test. You see, Grace knew about Ava's illness and wanted to protect herself," said Father Douglas, moving even nearer.

"Illness, what illness?" asked Addison, beginning to get that uneasy feeling again.

"For supposedly being such a great detective, you need to brush up on your powers of observation! Take a good look at your client," advised Father Douglas with a smirk.

Addison turned her head and looked at Ava. She had turned pale and was shaking badly. Her eyes were wild and glassy. Although her hands were at her sides, she kept clenching and unclenching her hands.

"What's wrong with her?" asked Addison as she turned back to the priest.

"Severe manic-depression. Grace told me that Ava's been in and out of hospitals for most of her life. She does pretty well for a time on medication, but then she goes off her meds and something triggers another episode. This time, it was finding her birth mother," answered Father Douglas.

"Then what was the real reason that Grace had been blackmailing you?" asked Addison, not sure if she wanted to know.

"Well, you see, Grace had read about the body found under the church bell tower in her local newspaper. It got her thinking and then she figured it out and came to Glendale with the express purpose of making me pay, literally, for what I had done," answered Father Douglas with a grin.

"What was it that you had done?" asked Addison with a terrible feeling that she already knew.

"Why, I murdered the 'love of her life,' what else?" replied Father Douglas with a queer look in his eyes.

Chapter 20

Ava shouted, "You're lying! My mother wouldn't lie to me. She loved me!"

Father Douglas laughed and said, "Your mother didn't love you, she only wanted you out of the way."

"How would you know how my mother felt about me?" demanded Ava, becoming even more agitated.

"She told me so during our meeting in the park the night she was murdered," answered Father Douglas with a calculated look.

Addison interjected, "So, you murdered Grace Evans because she was blackmailing you, didn't you?"

"Miss Temple, I hate to disappoint you, but Grace Evans was very much alive when I left her in the park that night. I had no intention of killing her then. My plan was to pick another more opportune moment that was less public," replied Father Douglas.

"Then, if you didn't kill her, do you know who did?" asked Addison.

Father Douglas looked at Addison, then looked at Ava and asked, "Why not ask your client? I would bet she followed Grace to the park that night and listened in on my meeting with her mother. How else would she have known what Grace had told me about her deceiving Ava regarding the identity of her father?"

Addison turned to look at Ava and knew the answer to his question. Ava's face had turned to one of pure hatred and vengeance. She looked crazed and out of control.

"Yes, I killed her. She was my mother and she should have loved me. I loved her! Why did she have to lie to me? I had to stop her from lying to me anymore," said Ava with a far-away look on her face.

Just as Father Douglas turned his eyes on Addison to gauge her reaction to Ava's admission of guilt, Ava attacked with the intensity that the mentally ill often possess. Father Douglas fired wildly, narrowly missing Ava as she ran into the darkness.

Addison took advantage of the distraction to lunge toward Father Douglas. Father Douglas yelled, "Take one more step and it will be your last!"

"You're just as crazy as Ava if you think you'll get away with this! Ava is out there somewhere," said Addison with as much conviction as she could gather.

"Ava is no threat to me, I'll take care of her later," said Father Douglas and motioned to Addison to walk in front of him toward the front of the church.

***

Father Douglas and Addison walked along the sidewalk that led to the front of the church, which also went by the fenced-off area around the bell tower. Addison hesitated and turned around to look at Father Douglas.

155

"Keep going, Miss Temple," demanded Father Douglas.

"What are you going to do?" asked Addison as she turned back to look at the hole at the base of the tower.

"I think it's usually referred to as the 'murderer returning to the scene of the crime' in mystery novels," replied Father Douglas as the front entrance lights shone on his face.

Addison saw the peculiar expression on his face and knew exactly what he meant.

"Move over to the edge of the hole, Miss Temple!" said Father Douglas behind her.

Addison slowly moved until she stood just inches from the edge of the black hole. With a swift push, she was plunging head-first into the darkness. She landed with a thud, luckily avoiding several large rocks at its bottom. Although she felt dazed and disoriented from the fall, she immediately began to feel her way along the side of the hole, hoping to find something she could use to escape.

Meanwhile, Father Douglas was standing at the top edge of the hole trying to pinpoint Addison's exact location. As he looked down into the dark hole, he heard the sound of the bulldozer coming to life, which had been left just a few feet away from the hole's edge.

He turned around quickly. In doing so, he lost his footing. In an instant, Father Douglas had joined his intended victim at the bottom. His robes entangled his feet so that when he landed, his left ankle twisted badly. He cried out in pain.

The sound of the bulldozer moved closer and closer. In moments, he felt a shower of gravel fall on his head and

156

shoulders. He looked up and saw the silhouette of someone on the machine. Then, he recognized the features of Ava Richardson. She was proceeding to bury them alive.

Chapter 21

Addison felt her way around the sides of the hole for something, anything that could function as a ladder for escape. There seemed no way to climb the sides of the hole. She felt panic begin to grip her.

Father Douglas got to his feet with a groan. He was relieved that his ankle hadn't broken, although what good it did, he really didn't know. How could he move to even attempt to get out of this hole? It occurred to him that Father Sebastian must have felt much like he felt right now—trapped and helpless. If only he had managed to hang on to his gun when he fell into the hole, he could try to land a shot on Ava when she made her next pass to dump more gravel. Now it was probably lying above him somewhere beyond reach.

The gravel kept raining down, filling in the hole bucketful by bucketful. Ava Richardson was relentless in her mission to kill them both. The constant drone of the bulldozer's engine rang in his ears. Father Douglas yelled out to Addison, "Miss Temple, where are you? I can't move, I think I've sprained my ankle."

Addison shouted back, "I'm over here to your right. I can't find a way out!"

The gravel was now reaching their knees and it was getting harder and harder to avoid being hit by each bucketful. They both started screaming for help, but the sound of the engine drowned out their cries.

***

Logan Stanton drove like a man possessed as he made his way to the Our Lady of the Lake Catholic Church. It seemed like he would never get there. He kept thinking over and over about what Sam Richardson had told him about Ava's sickness and the blackmail scheme. How did Grace Evans fit into everything? What about Father Douglas? Where did he come into the picture? Why hadn't he mentioned that he had been assigned more than once to the Our Lady of the Lakes Catholic Church? Why did his mind keep returning to the photograph of the three kids? Was Father Douglas the second boy in the photograph? Was he connected to Father Sebastian's murder as well as Grace Evans's murder? Or, had Ava Richardson murdered her mother? And if so, why?

He purposefully put these questions out of his mind, focusing on finding Addison as soon as he could and, hopefully, saving her from any potential harm, or worse. He tried not to think about the 'worse,' it clouded his judgment. Right now, he needed all his senses working at their best.

He finally turned onto Abbey Street, which led to the Catholic Church. To his surprise, someone was operating the bulldozer. Why would someone use a bulldozer at this time of the evening? Then, a terrible thought entered his mind and he screeched to a halt and jumped out of his car and ran across the front lawn. Logan reached the bell tower area and looked up into the dozer's cab. He could make out a figure sitting behind the controls.

He pulled out his gun, then began shouting and waving frantically. Finally, the operator spotted him; however, instead of stopping, the operator changed direction and headed straight for him. Logan dodged the bulldozer and managed to grab on to the cab's door handle, yanking it open.

Meanwhile, the gravel had already reached the shoulders of Addison and Father Douglas. They were having trouble staying above the surface as the gravel shifted each time Ava had dumped another bucketful over the edge of the hole. Gravel and dirt particles covered their faces and filled their mouths and noses. When they heard the noise of the engine recede for a few minutes, they couldn't help clinging to the faint hope that someone had come to rescue them.

***

Logan recognized Ava Richardson by the interior lights illuminating the cab. He remembered seeing a photo of her 6+in Chief McGraw's case. He tried to reach across to the ignition in order to yank out the key. Ava fought like a wild thing, beating and scratching him. Finding it impossible to get his hand on the key, he began pulling Ava forcibly out of the cab. While they struggled, one of Ava's hands touched on a wrench on the floor beside her. She grabbed it

160

and swung at Logan, narrowly missing the side of his head. The attack gave her enough time to jump out of the dozer, which, by now, had stalled.

Logan jumped out of the cab and ran after her. Ava stumbled, falling to the ground as she tried to get away. As she got to her feet, she saw the gun that Father Douglas must have dropped when he fell into the hole. Grabbing it, Ava turned and pointed it at Logan who was gaining on her. She shot; Logan fell. He did not move. In a moment, Ava was again inside the bulldozer and moving in the direction of the hole.

Chapter 22

The sound broke through his consciousness. He couldn't figure it out. Where was it coming from? Logan opened his eyes. The bulldozer! He tried to stand, then looked down at his left leg. His pant leg was covered with blood and more was seeping through. Ava's shot had struck his left upper thigh.

Once more, he tried to stand and fell again. Each time he tried; the stream of blood grew. He could see Ava at the wheel of the dozer dumping more gravel into the hole. Logan started dragging himself toward the machine. He didn't even think about what he was going to do once he reached it; he just knew he had to get there.

Ava reversed the dozer and turned it toward the pile of gravel. By doing so, she turned in Logan's direction. Her face froze. He was still alive! She reached for the gun on the seat and started shooting. Ava was not an accomplished marksman, much to Logan's advantage. The movement of the dozer did not help either. Her shot struck the ground behind him and to the right. He kept on moving. Ava tried to shoot again, but her hands were shaking. The gun jammed.

In desperation, Ava threw the gun at Logan. In doing so, she hit the controls beside her. The dozer started circling wildly, out of control. Ava began pulling at the controls, trying to stop it. Its circle grew wider until finally, the dozer hit the edge of the gravel pile, causing it to tip over on its side. Ava's short-lived career as a bulldozer operator had ended abruptly since she had just been pinned beneath the 8-ton D3 Caterpillar dozer.

***

Logan watched the bulldozer's erratic movements and prayed that it did not head in his direction. When he saw it tip over and pin Ava beneath, he wasted no time. He kept on crawling until he reached the hole and looked down.

His heart stood still. There was no sign of life. What was once a deep, gaping hole was now nearly completely filled in with fresh gravel. He crawled into what was left of the hole. The lights from the overturned bulldozer shone brightly into the hole. He started shouting, "Addison, where are you? Addison! Addison! It's Logan, show me where you are!"

He started digging with his hands, trying to find her. He had no idea how long she had been buried. It could already be too late, but he had to try. As he dug, he suddenly noticed a piece of pipe poking straight up through the gravel toward one side. Frantically, he started digging around the pipe. He dug for what seemed like hours, but in reality, was only seconds.

Suddenly, he felt something that felt soft. It was hair, Addison's hair. His desperation turned to panic. He may not be too late if Addison was using the pipe to breathe. His hands felt her face, then her neck. He made the hole wider and exposed her head and shoulders. He brushed off her eyes, nose, and mouth. "Addison, say something—please, say something," he cried.

She opened her eyes and looked at him. Tears ran down her dirty cheeks, leaving tiny, wet streaks of mud. "Logan," she whispered.

"Father Douglas. He's beside me. Had a pipe too, maybe already covered, find him," Addison whispered again before passing out.

***

The night air was suddenly filled with the sounds of police sirens, which grew louder and louder. Tires screeched as a half dozen of Glendale's finest drew up to the Our Lady of the Lake Catholic Church on that fateful night. The Glendale Hospital Ambulance was not far behind.

Chief McGraw arrived minutes later. For the first time in what had been a very long time, he was seen running to the scene of a crime. As he neared the scene, he saw the overturned bulldozer. "What's going on?" he asked of one of his officers breathlessly.

Officer Reynolds replied, "Chief, a body of a woman was just pulled out from under the dozer. It's too late for her, I'm afraid the only place she's going is the morgue. Three people are being loaded into the ambulance now. We found two of them—a man and a woman who had been buried beneath the bell tower along with that detective,

Logan Stanton who has a leg wound and has lost a lot of blood."

Chief McGraw stood speechless for a few seconds, then walked toward the ambulance. With some difficulty, he recognized Addison Temple. Then his gaze shifted to the man who was obviously a priest judging from the dirt-covered robes on his body. He reached in and wiped away some dirt still on the man's face; the man's eyes opened and blinked at him. The chief drew in his breath, it was Father Douglas.

Then, McGraw turned to the man on the stretcher next to the ambulance. Emergency personnel surrounded him. Quickly, they loaded him into the ambulance. The doors closed behind all three of them and then they were gone.

Chief McGraw stood there for a very long time. Retirement seemed such a very long time away.

Chapter 23

Olivia Temple got off the elevator on the fourth floor of the Glendale Hospital and walked down the corridor toward the nurse's station with all the outward appearance of someone on a mission. Her 'baby' was on this floor and needed her mother and no one was going to stop her from going to her. She reached the desk and addressed the nurse on duty, "I'm Olivia Temple, my daughter was just brought in and I was told she is on this floor. I must see her right away. Which room is she in?" asked Olivia without pausing for breath.

The nurse looked up from the chart she was reading and replied, "You must mean Addison Temple. The doctor is in with her now but should be out in just a few minutes. Please have a chair in the waiting area and I will let him know you're here."

"Don't you understand? I must see her immediately! I insist on seeing her!" exclaimed Olivia, her voice rising.

The nurse looked at her calmly. She had dealt with family members like this before. "I'm sorry, Mrs. Temple, but your daughter is with the doctor and cannot be disturbed right now. I'm sure it will be just a few minutes and you will be able to see her," she answered with an understanding look.

Unfortunately for the nurse on duty that day, she was not acquainted with Olivia Temple. If she had been, she would have known that Olivia Temple did not take being told 'no' in an understanding manner, nor did she appreciate being treated as if she were a typical, overbearing mother. Overbearing, yes—typical, never!

Olivia Temple opened her mouth to provide the nurse with a lecture on the rights of motherhood, then decided to forego it in favor of the 'direct' approach. Instead, she said in the most 'understanding' voice she could manage, "I understand, of course. Would you please give me her room number so that I may at least send her some flowers?"

The nurse thought to herself, *I knew I could handle her,* and replied, "Of course, Mrs. Temple, she is in Room 410."

Olivia turned from the desk and started down the hall that appeared most likely to have Room 410. The nurse was stunned. The next moment, she was on her feet and running after Olivia Temple, calling out, "Mrs. Temple, come back here!"

Olivia was not stopping for anyone, least of all a nurse with an attitude. For you see, there were very few people with more attitude than Oliva Temple! She finally came to Room 410 and was about to turn the door handle when someone came up beside her and put an arm around her. She looked up and there stood Farley Brooks. He smiled and asked quietly, "Mrs. Temple, won't you wait with me and have a cup of coffee?"

Olivia looked startled, then confused, and finally, slightly flustered. "Mr. Brooks, I had no idea you were here.

Of course, you would be here, wouldn't you? I am sure you are very concerned about Addison, as we all are," said Olivia, looking accusingly at the nurse who appeared out of breath, but ready to stand her ground no matter what came her way.

Farley took Olivia's hand in his and led her to the waiting area. "Please sit down. May I get you a cup of coffee?" he asked gently.

Olivia nodded and sat down. "That would be very nice, thank you."

Soon Farley returned with two cups of coffee and handed one to Olivia and sat down beside her. "Please don't worry, Mrs. Temple, I'm sure Addison will be just fine in a few days," he said with a smile.

Olivia managed a smile of her own. "You're very kind, Mr. Brooks," she answered, taking a sip from her cup. She noticed for the first time how attractive Farley Brooks really was. His silver hair really became him. He was certainly anything but 'typical' himself!

"May I call you Olivia?" asked Farley as he smiled, looking into her eyes.

Olivia smiled back and replied, "Only if I may call you Farley."

The nurse couldn't quite conceal her surprise when she walked over a few minutes later to inform them that the doctor and patient were available now. Mrs. Temple and Mr. Brooks were holding hands, oblivious to the world around them.

***

Addison looked at herself in her compact and frowned. Although a shower had done wonders, it could not remove the bruises and cuts on her face and neck that had resulted from her ordeal. She was just applying some powder and lipstick when her hospital room door opened and in stepped none other than Jackson Smythe carrying a large bouquet of red roses. He smiled and entered.

Addison tried to force a smile; however, she winced when her face hurt at the movement. Jackson bent over her, kissing her long and tenderly. Addison succumbed to his embrace but couldn't help comparing his kiss to one she had experienced not all that long ago.

"How are you, darling? I was so worried when I heard what happened. I had to come and see you as soon as they would let me!" said Jackson, handing her the roses.

"Thank you, Jackson, the flowers are lovely," replied Addison, motioning him to sit in the chair beside her bed, "I'm fine, just bruised a bit. The doctor thinks I can go home in a couple of days or so."

"What good news! How about I take you home when the time comes? I'm going to take good care of you from now on, darling, you can count on it!" said Jackson, reaching for her hand.

Addison looked down at her hand in his and remembered another hand that had held hers in a similar fashion. Somehow, it just wasn't the same this time.

***

Chief McGraw walked up to the Glendale Hospital reception desk and spoke to the receptionist on duty. She pointed to the elevator to the right of the desk. He nodded and walked to it with his customary shuffle and pushed 'Up.' The elevator doors opened, he entered, and pushed number four. He was not smiling as the door closed upon his formidable form.

Upon reaching the fourth floor, Chief McGraw shuffled down the corridor toward Room 420. When he reached it, he knocked and entered as quietly as he could.

Logan Stanton lay on his hospital bed with his left leg elevated. He woke as the chief entered the room. He smiled and said, "Good morning, Chief! How's tricks?"

Chief McGraw forced a smirk and said, "For a man who was nearly killed last night, you sure are chipper this morning."

"Why shouldn't I be? With Addison Temple's help, I was able to crack a 30-year-old cold case and solve a second, related case to boot. In addition, and might I add, more importantly, I saved the life of the most beautiful and fascinating women I have ever had the privilege to meet in the process!" replied Logan with an even broader smile.

The chief looked at him with some surprise. If he didn't know better, he would say the Logan Stanton was in love. Unbelievable! "Just so you know, Stanton, that if it hadn't been for the passer-by who happened to hear the shots, you would probably not be alive today!" he said with a self-important look.

"Of course, Chief, you are absolutely correct. I owe my life to you and your department," responded Logan, trying to conceal his amusement.

Chief McGraw looked at Logan sharply to see if he was poking fun at him. Not quite sure, he decided to give him the benefit of the doubt and press on. "We'll need a full statement from you and Miss Temple just as soon as you both are able to do so," he said as he took out his pocket notebook to make a few preliminary notes.

"I'm sure Miss Temple and I would be happy to provide any information that you require," answered Logan, trying to ease his wounded leg into a more comfortable position.

"Speaking of Miss Temple, what room is she in?" asked the chief, writing in his notebook.

Logan opened his mouth to answer when the door opened and in walked Jackson Smythe pushing Addison Temple in a wheelchair. Addison was looking beautiful as usual, although slightly bruised from her ordeal. A good night's sleep and a shower had done wonders! Logan looked at her and silently thanked God for saving her life. She must never know how close she had come to death last night. Then, he shifted his gaze to Jackson Smythe and did not pretend to like what he saw. "Morning, Smythe. You're here bright and early!" greeted Logan with a trace of sarcasm in his voice.

Jackson noted the sarcasm and Logan's expression; decided to take full advantage, he replied, "Good morning, Stanton. You seem just like your old self despite your recent brush with death."

Logan proceeded to ignore him and turned his attention to the beautiful woman seated in the wheelchair. "How are you this morning?" asked Logan, smiling at her.

Addison smiled, although her face hurt at the motion. She replied, "I am much better, thank you."

Chief McGraw walked over to her wheelchair and held out his hand. Addison looked at him, then shook his hand.

He said, "I want to thank you personally for all the work you did on these cases, Miss Temple, and I'm glad you made it OK."

Addison stared at him, wondering if she had heard correctly or not. She hesitated a moment and then said quietly, "You are welcome, Chief."

"Chief, how is Father Douglas doing?" asked Logan.

Chief McGraw shook his head, "The doctor is not sure at this point; all I can tell you is that his condition is stable, but we should know more in the next 24 hours or so. In any event, he will remain under guard at the hospital until he can be moved to jail."

Logan and Addison looked at each other with a knowing look. They knew the case wouldn't be closed until they cleared up some unfinished business with Father Douglas.

***

A couple of days later, Addison Temple walked into the Glendale Hospital under her own steam. She looked nearly back to her usual self. She had decided on a more feminine approach today and had dressed in a simple, but lovely gray suit of a classic cut with matching shoes. She had carefully applied makeup to try to camouflage the bruises that remained on her face and neck.

She walked straight to the elevator that would take her to the fourth floor, pushed the button, and waited. When she was inside, she smiled as the elevator rose. It would be great to see Logan again. She owed him her life. But she had no more time to think about Logan Stanton because no sooner had the elevator stopped than the man himself was seated in a wheelchair looking at her. She looked startled, then pleased to see him. Unfortunately, her pleasure quickly turned to disappointment when she saw who was standing behind the chair poised to push Logan into the elevator. Chelsea Matthews, looking very attractive in a rather seductively-cut red dress that showed off her figure to perfection, stared at her, clearly annoyed at who she saw staring back at her from within the elevator. Addison managed a nod and a "Good morning" at the woman who responded likewise.

On the other hand, Logan's eyes lit up at seeing Addison and smiled appreciatively at the sight of her. "I was hoping you would drop by to see me soon," was all he said.

Addison looked down at him, smiled, and said, "I wanted to see how you are coming along."

"I'm doing much better. We probably shouldn't keep the elevator on this floor. I was on my way down to see Father Douglas. The chief informed me he was doing better and would be allowed questioning. I'm sure you want to be there too," replied Logan with one of his most charming smiles.

Addison moved aside so that he and his escort could get on the elevator and returned his smile. "What do you think?" she asked.

***

Addison, along with Logan seated in his wheelchair, made their way past the armed guard into Father Douglas's hospital room. Thankfully for Addison, but to Chelsea's frustration, the guard had prohibited her from accompanying them.

Logan and Addison didn't know quite what to expect as they moved into the room.

Father Douglas was asleep on his bed. The television played in the background. He awoke as soon as they entered and stared at them both. "Well, I didn't expect to see you two," was all he said. He looked tired. Like Addison, his face and neck were bruised from the gravel and the ordeal of being buried alive.

"How are you doing?" asked Logan as they moved closer to him.

"As well as can be expected after being buried alive. The doctor tells me that I will be recovered enough to be moved to the city jail tomorrow. I suppose I should be grateful to both of you for saving my life," answered Father Douglas, looking grim.

"Well, the use of the pipes was Miss Temple's idea. She's the one who actually saved your life—I only followed her instructions about where to look for you," replied Logan with a grin.

Addison thought back to the recent hellish ordeal. "We need to clarify a couple of points with you, Father, if you are up to it," she said.

"Do I have a choice?" asked Father Douglas with a blank look in his eyes.

"You admitted to killing your childhood friend and fellow priest, Father Sebastian, all those years ago; however, we are curious about your motive. You said something about murdering Grace Evans's 'love of her life.' Was it jealousy that prompted you to murder Father

Sebastian because you were also in love with Grace, although she preferred Father Sebastian over you?" asked Addison, leaning forward in anticipation of his answer.

Father Douglas looked at her for a moment in silence. Then he said with a touch of malice in his voice, "Miss Temple, as I said before, what kind of detective are you anyway? I would have thought you might have considered some other motive than the obvious one of a 'lover scorned!'"

Addison and Logan looked at each other. Logan asked abruptly, "Come out with it. What are you talking about?"

Father Douglas smiled; however, the smile didn't quite make it to his eyes. He replied, "Father Sebastian and I were not only childhood friends, but we share another relationship as well."

Addison looked at Logan and then asked the priest, "What do you mean, another relationship?"

Father Douglas shifted himself to a more comfortable position. He winced at the pain of movement. He looked at them both and shook his head in disbelief and said, "Haven't either of you done any investigation into the childhood of Father Sebastian and myself? Apparently, my prior question regarding Miss Temple's detective ability applies to both of you!"

"Would you just come out with it?" responded Logan in a very frustrated voice.

"Well, since you ask so graciously, I will," answered Father Douglas with a definite sneer on his 'not-so-priestly' face.

"Father Sebastian and I were half-brothers. We both had the same mother, but different fathers. Our mother was first married to Father Sebastian's father; however, they divorced shortly after he was born. She then married my father and I was born a short while later," explained Father Douglas with a very faraway look in his eyes.

"Mother always favored Sebastian and enjoyed setting us against each other. You see, our mother was mentally ill. Her illness became even more pronounced as the years went by. Where do you think Ava Richardson's mental illness came from? She enjoyed the distinction of being born into the third generation of mentally ill in the family," he continued in a voice devoid of any emotion.

"Mother also began to drink heavily. By the time we were about to graduate from high school, she was a full-blown alcoholic," added Father Douglas.

"One day, Mother wanted to go to the liquor store a few blocks away from our home. She had run out of whiskey and needed more. When I refused to drive her, she asked Sebastian. She knew exactly how to manipulate him into doing whatever she wanted. Naturally, he said yes," said Father Douglas in the same expressionless tone.

"I warned Sebastian that he shouldn't go. He had been drinking just like our mother. He laughed and refused to listen. You see, he was much like our mother and I believe he had managed to inherit some mental illness tendencies of his very own from her," explained the priest, watching their reactions.

"Mother and Sebastian left for the liquor store in his old 'beater' of a car. About a half-hour later, the phone rang. It was the police. They told me that Mother's car had hit a telephone pole, but that she was still alive and in an ambulance on her way to the hospital," said Father Douglas, turning his gaze to the window beside his bed.

There was silence for several seconds while Father Douglas relived once again those moments all those years ago. Finally, he turned to look at them and said, "When the police called, they informed me that our mother was behind the wheel of the car when they found her."

Both Addison and Logan looked at each other and then back at the priest. Addison was the first to speak, "Wasn't Sebastian the driver of the car when the two of them left the house?"

Father Douglas replied with a short, hard laugh, "Finally, some definite indication that you are a 'real' detective, Miss Temple! You are indeed correct. For you see, my dear half-brother had moved our mother over behind the wheel after the accident because he didn't want another DWI since it would have been his second offense. He knew Mother was unconscious but didn't think her injuries were that serious. He fled the scene and only later learned she had died on the way to the hospital. That's when he panicked because then he knew that he would have been charged with vehicular homicide if he had been found out."

Logan interjected, "But you knew that Sebastian had been the driver. Why didn't you tell the police?"

Father Douglas smiled rather sadly, "Call it 'brotherly love' or call it 'stupidity.' Either way, I didn't want our family name to be dragged through the mud. When Sebastian pleaded with me not to tell the police that he had been the driver and that he had been drunk, I agreed to lie for him."

Addison was almost out of her chair with anticipation. She asked quickly, "Then what happened?"

Father Douglas stared at them for a few seconds and then replied, "Sebastian had become consumed with guilt. That's when he gave up drinking and enrolled in the seminary. He somehow thought priesthood would be a way to relieve his guilt and atone for what he had done."

No one said anything for several moments. Addison broke the silence first when she asked, "You are telling us that you murdered Father Sebastian because he was driving the car at the time of the accident that killed your mother?"

"Precisely, Miss Temple. He was responsible for our mother's death. I told him I would get even with him someday. He never wanted me to have her love when she was alive. He made sure I would never have it when he killed her. I wasn't going to let him get away with it," replied Father Douglas with conviction.

"But why did you wait until after you both had completed seminary school before you killed Sebastian?" asked Logan with a puzzled look.

Father Douglas looked at him with a quizzical look and asked, "Mr. Stanton, hasn't it occurred to you that I, too, may have inherited mental illness from our mother? I have also been diagnosed with manic depression and have experienced the 'highs' and the 'lows' of the illness. However, my diagnosis did not take place until later in life. It was during one of the 'lows' that my depression overcame me to the point that I sought revenge for my mother's death."

Both Addison and Logan looked at each other.

Father Douglas went on in a monotone voice, "Sebastian had worked hard at his studies, and becoming a priest meant a great deal to him. His reasons for becoming a priest were not pure ones. He thought he could make up for his past sins. I wanted him to know what it feels like to have something in reach, but never be able to have it just like he had made me feel about mother's love for me," replied Father Douglas with a distorted look.

Then Logan asked, "Was Father Sebastian the real father of Ava Richardson?"

Father Douglas stared out of the window and did not answer. Logan was about to repeat the question when suddenly, Father Douglas turned to look at them and said, "Yes, Father Sebastian was Ava's father. Grace learned she was pregnant after he had begun his studies at the seminary. She never told him because she didn't want the child. I was the only one who knew."

Chapter 24

A few days later, Logan Stanton lay on his couch dozing in the afternoon sunshine. His leg had improved to the point of only needing a walking stick to get around. Suddenly, the tranquility of this cozy scene was interrupted by the shrill sound of his apartment doorbell. *Damn!* He had finally got comfortable and now someone had to disturb him.

With some difficulty, he managed to stand up and reach for his stick. The doorbell rang again. "Just a minute, please!" called Logan as he made his way slowly toward the door.

He reached the door and yanked it open. Much to his surprise, there stood the one person he really had not expected to see—Chelsea Matthews!

"Well, hello Chelsea. This is indeed a surprise!" said Logan as his frown turned into one of his "signature" smiles.

"Hello, Logan, I hope I'm not disturbing you?" asked Chelsea as she took the liberty of walking past him into the apartment.

"Of course not, Chelsea; do come in, won't you?" replied Logan with a touch of sarcasm noting she was already "in."

"I just had to come and see you after I heard you had been released from the hospital a few days ago. I've been so worried about you!" said Chelsea as she walked across to the couch he had just vacated and sat down. She strategically placed herself in a position that would reveal the length of her long, slim legs to perfection while the soft yellow knit dress she wore clung to her curves.

Logan watched her movements with some amusement. No doubt about it, Chelsea was on the 'prowl' and he was quite sure he was the intended target! He moved slowly across to her and sat down beside her.

Chelsea took his hand and moved closer to him. He could smell her perfume. It seemed to wrap itself around him. He had forgotten how sexy she was. He had a feeling she was about to remind him.

"Can I get you anything? I've got some coffee made, or maybe you would rather have some tea?" asked Logan as he slowly pulled his hand away.

"I would love some tea but let me make it. Don't get up. I think I remember where you keep things in your kitchen," she replied with a smile as she stood up and disappeared into the kitchen.

Logan followed her with his eyes. Yes, Chelsea Matthews was definitely out to get him. Suddenly, his leg started hurting and he felt very tired, and just a little bored. If he would have been totally honest with himself, he might have been able to identify yet another feeling—guilt.

***

Two weeks later, Logan—with a bouquet of roses in one hand and a cane in the other—stood in front of Addison's apartment door. He pushed the buzzer with the tip of his cane and waited. He heard footsteps and the door opened.

Addison opened the door and smiled. "Hi, come in. You shouldn't be on your feet for too long."

Logan smiled and handed her the roses, "Hi beautiful, these are for you."

She helped him to the couch and said, "I'll just be a minute, I want to put these into water. They're lovely; thank you so much, Logan."

"I'm glad you like them," said Logan as he watched her select a vase from a cabinet and fill it at the kitchen sink. She was wearing a soft mauve-colored dress cut low in the back, which exposed her neck and back as she worked at the sink.

"How are you doing? It looks like you're getting around quite well. Are you almost back to your normal activity?" she asked as she carried the vase to the living room. She placed it in the center of the coffee table and sat down beside him.

"I've been doing more and more. The doctor says I should be able to get rid of this cane in a few days. I'm back in the office, but I'm not able to do much investigative work quite yet," replied Logan, pointing down at his leg.

"Are you sure you should be even going back to the office yet? That was a bad gunshot wound you had," said Addison with a concerned look.

"I can't just sit around doing nothing. I've got to keep busy and work is all I've got, or I should say, had," said Logan as he reached for her hand, looking into her eyes.

Addison's eyes widened and seemed to turn an even deeper green as her gaze locked with his. "Logan, I don't know how to thank you for saving my life. If it weren't for you, I wouldn't be here today," she said as tears formed in her eyes.

Logan reached up and wiped away a tear that had spilled out down her cheek. Then, he leaned over to her and softly caressed her lips with his own.

***

That evening, they enjoyed a lovely dinner at Mario's, a popular Italian restaurant in town. The wine, the service, and the company were perfect. Other patrons in the restaurant couldn't help noticing the very attractive couple seated in a secluded corner booth who had eyes only for each other. No one or nothing else seemed to matter. Of course, they couldn't resist talking 'shop' over their dinner.

"Logan, how did you know that Father Douglas was the third person in the photograph?" asked Addison curiously.

Logan leaned forward and explained, "Actually, there were a couple of clues. First, the church board chairman revealed that Father Douglas had two assignments with the Our Lady of the Lake Catholic Church, not just the present one, which was something that Father Douglas failed to mention to me when I spoke with him. The second clue that tipped me off was Father Douglas's degree certificate from seminary school. I happened to notice it was signed by the same person who had signed Father Sebastian's certificate. Father Douglas had changed the name of the seminary along with the date because he didn't want anyone to know he had known Father Sebastian. That way, there would be no possible way to link him to Father Sebastian's disappearance."

Logan reached for Addison's hand and continued, "I can't even imagine what it must have felt like to be buried alive!"

Addison shuddered and said, "I don't even want to think about it. It was the worst experience of my life. I thought I was going to die."

Logan smiled at her and said, "But, you didn't because you kept your wits about you. That's what makes you such a good detective."

"I don't think I was such a good detective. If I were, I would have been able to figure out that Ava Richardson was manic-depressive. Looking back, I should have realized her mood changes were not normal," replied Addison with a frown.

"Don't beat yourself up over it," responded Logan. "We all miss things sometimes. The important thing is that by working together, we were able to solve not just one murder case, but two!"

Addison asked, "Do you think Father Joseph's last words, 'He shouldn't have been a priest' referred to Father Sebastian or not?"

Logan shrugged his shoulders and answered, "I'm not sure. I don't think we'll ever know. Father Sebastian was the father of an illegitimate child, left the scene of an accident, and was guilty of vehicular manslaughter, while

Father Douglas committed murder. None of these actions can be considered 'priestly.'"

Addison thought about it for a few seconds and then remarked quietly, "Has it occurred to you that Father Douglas, rather than Father Sebastian, was really the father of Ava Richardson?"

They both stared at each other in disbelief. Logan finally spoke, "Do you mean to tell me that you believe Father Douglas and Father Sebastian both had sex with Grace Evans when they were teenagers and either one could have been the father?"

Addison slowly nodded her head and said excitedly. "I think it's a definite angle we hadn't considered until now. Father Douglas could be lying to us and maybe he wanted Grace himself and killed Father Sebastian out of jealousy and not to get even with him for killing their mother as he said!"

Logan dropped the fork he had been using to spear the last of his salad and exclaimed, "Then Ava's mental illness could have come from her grandmother by way of Father Douglas or Father Sebastian!"

"You got it!" answered Addison with flushed cheeks. "How will we know what Father Douglas's motive really was? And, not to mention, who really was Ava Richardson's father?" Excitement shone in her green eyes, causing them to positively sparkle in the dim light of the restaurant.

They didn't say anything for a very long time. Both were deep in thought. Finally, Logan said with one of his customary grins, "Well, since Father Sebastian, Grace Evans, and Ava Richardson are all dead, and Father

Douglas will be tried for the murder of Father Sebastian, the answers to those questions may never be known. I don't think the court will be interested in a DNA test on Father Douglas in order to establish the paternity of a deceased Ava Richardson. Father Douglas's confession to the murder will seal his fate and most likely land him behind bars for the rest of his life. He will have plenty of time to think about the real reason he murdered his half-brother and childhood friend."

Addison was clearly disappointed. Her eyes had lost their sparkle and had turned a deep emerald green. Then she smiled suddenly and said, "Well, we know there's one thing that Father Douglas did not lie about!"

Logan smiled back and answered, "Don't tell me, let me guess!"

He thought for a moment, then, suddenly he laughed out loud and pronounced, "I know. *Neither* of us is very much of a detective!"

Then they raised their wine glasses and toasted this amazing revelation!

***

Addison drove Logan's car back to her apartment since his leg had started to hurt. He had protested, but she had not taken 'no' for an answer. As he sat next to her, he felt what he could only describe as a 'flutter' inside him. She touched his heart in a way no other woman had ever done. He knew there was only one word for it.

As they sat on the couch drinking their coffee, Logan said, "Addison, can I ask you something?"

She looked up from her cup and said carefully, "Of course, you can ask me anything." She couldn't help wondering just what it was he was going to ask her.

"I was wondering—since we obviously demonstrated that we work well together—would you consider working with me on some other cases that may come along?" asked Logan, trying not to appear too hopeful.

Addison suddenly felt somehow disappointed. Then, she shook herself mentally and snapped back to her 'old self.' *Why did she allow this man to affect her so? This has just got to stop, or she wasn't Addison Temple!* Out loud, she said, "I would like nothing better, Logan."

They decided to officially seal the bargain with a kiss.

The End